# Yosele

## A Story from Jewish Life

# Yosele

## A Story from Jewish Life

### Jacob Dinezon

Translated from the Yiddish by
### Jane Peppler

Foreword by
### Scott Hilton Davis

Published by
Jewish Storyteller Press
2015

Edited by Scott Hilton Davis

Cover illustration from the painting
"Young Jewish Boy" by Wilhelm Wachtel

Translated from
*Yosele: Dertseylung fun Yidishn Lebn*
Yakov Dinezon
Hebrew Publishing Company, New York, 1923

Published by Jewish Storyteller Press
Raleigh, North Carolina, U.S.A.
www.jewishstorytellerpress.com
books@jewishstorytellerpress.com

Printed in the United States

Learn more about Jacob Dinezon at www.jacobdinezon.com

ISBN 978-0-9798156-3-8

Library of Congress Control Number: 2014945525

For our dedicated *kindershul* and *mitlshul* teachers, who, unlike Berl the *Melamed*, lovingly taught us to revere Yiddish, *yidishkayt*, and Jewish culture.

# FOREWORD

This is not an easy book to read. The depiction of violence against a young schoolboy is harsh and startling. It is distressing to think that such things went on in the Jewish communities of Eastern Europe. Yet, like the works of Charles Dickens, which described the cruel treatment of children in mid-nineteenth century England, Jacob Dinezon presents, in unflinching detail, the social issues facing shtetl society at the turn of the twentieth century.

Writing in Yiddish to reach the broadest Jewish audience, Dinezon challenged his readers to face and address the injustices brought on by economic inequality and community indifference. And it is clear in this first-time English translation by Jane Peppler that Dinezon pulled no punches. His descriptions of poverty and physical abuse are brutal and heartbreaking.

By the time this novella was published in 1899, Jacob Dinezon was already a popular author who was known for his love of the Jewish people. In his prior works, Dinezon had tackled other difficult issues of his day, including arranged marriages, the disparities between rich and poor, and the clashes between Jewish tradition and modernity.

In *Yosele* (*Little Joseph*), Dinezon takes on the current state of cheder (elementary school) education with its often violent methods of teaching. The story describes in painfully descriptive language the tragic life of a bright and gentle boy who is born into poverty and relentlessly battered by family, school, and society.

Writing with heartfelt pathos, Jacob Dinezon vividly portrays the harsh conditions of life in the *shtetlach*, the Jewish towns and villages of Russia and Eastern Europe at the turn of the twentieth century. As the literary historian A. A. Roback points out in *The Story of Yiddish Literature*, "If we recall the children characters in Dickens' novels, like *Oliver Twist*, *Nicholas Nickleby*, and *David Copperfield*, and combine them, we should then obtain a slight idea of the sufferings little Yosele had undergone because of his poverty, misunderstandings, false accusations, etc."[1]

Other writers, including Mendele Moykher Sforim in *Dos Kleine Mentshele* (*The Little Man*), had decried the cruel treatment of schoolboys in the traditional Jewish elementary school of the late 1800s, but the publication of *Yosele* produced an urgent and dramatic call for change. The literary biographer Samuel Rozshanski wrote that the book was held up as a critique of the old-fashioned cheder system and "seemed to all preachers of modern Jewish education as a true picture of the class division that had been built up in Jewish life in the nineteenth century, and as an urging for fundamental educational reform in order to place it on a foundation of fairness and goodness. *Yosele* was taken in like a textbook in all Jewish folk-schools. A series of dramatizations of the whole book or of different chapters were acted on stage, especially by students on school holidays. Many stagings were used as the material for social discussions in newspapers, journals, lectures, and conferences by radical movements."[2]

The emotional impact of the story is reflected in an essay by one of I. L. Peretz's young protégés, Isaiah Trunk, who remembered *Yosele* as "a book over which I had wept a sea of tears. My mother had wailed aloud over it, and even hard-hearted Grandfather Boruch, reading it, had broken into sobs, and had groped for a cane to beat up Berl the cruel *melamed* (teacher)."[3]

Yet as painful and heartrending as the story is, Yiddish literary critic, Bal-Makhshoves (Israel Isidor Eliashev) suggests that Dinezon provides the reader with a glimmer of hope: "No matter how sad and unfortunate the circumstances of the individual's life should be, Dinezon still finds people and hearts that bring grace and light feeling into an individual's darkness and will at least lighten his last minutes while saying goodbye to the world."

With the appearance of a water carrier, teacher, and butcher late in the story, writes Bal-Makhshoves, "It seems to us a stone is removed from our hearts. In these three people, then, one hears the pulse of big, pure hearts full of love for people, for every individual, and we say to ourselves: where one can find a person like Yoyne the Water Carrier or Reb Shoyel the Butcher, there is still hope, still a belief that the life of a poor Jewish child will not always be so dark and bitter."[4]

Later in his life, Dinezon would become an ardent advocate for children's aid and education. In 1915, during World War One, Dinezon and his close friend I. L. Peretz founded an orphanage in Warsaw. This was acknowledged by the Warsaw newspaper, *Haynt*, at the time of Dinezon's death: "Dinezon was one of the first who, in the dark days of the expulsions when the streets of Warsaw were flooded with the homeless, began to rescue the children, establishing foster homes and schools to which he devoted himself heart and soul. To the hundreds of children who were educated in his foster homes he was literally a father."[5]

His deep concern for the proper education of children, says Sol Liptzin in *The Flowering of Yiddish*, led Dinezon "to pioneer the founding of a new, secular type of elementary Jewish school in which the traditional harsh method of the cat-o'-nine tails was replaced by kindness, understanding, and the stimulation of joyousness in the classroom. Such schools, which flourished during the First World War, were often called the Dinezon Schools. They persisted until the Nazi avalanche."[6]

In the end, Jacob Dinezon was honored for his efforts to improve Jewish education and for his kind and generous heart. What began as a heartbreaking tale of a poor Jewish boy trying to survive the violent treatment of a cruel teacher resulted in the exposé, outrage, and reform of the Jewish elementary school system. *Yosele*, by Jacob Dinezon, was a small book that profoundly changed the Jewish world.

# Notes

1   A. A. Roback, *The Story of Yiddish Literature*, Gordon Press: NY, 1974, pp. 161-163.

2   Jacob Dinezon, *Yosele. The Crisis: Novels and Studies on the Jewish Literature*, introduction by Samuel Rozshanski, Jane Peppler, translator, Yosef Lifshits-fond beim kultur-kongres in Argentina, Buenos-Ayres, 1959.

3   Jehiel Isaiah Trunk, L. Dawidowicz, translator, "Peretz at Home," *Three Great Classic Writers of Yiddish Literature: Selected Works of I. L. Peretz*, Marvin Zuckerman and Marion Herbst, editors, Joseph Simon Pangloss Press, CA, 1996, pp. 64-71.

4   Israel Isidor Eliashev, Jane Peppler, translator, "Jacob Dinezon," *The Gathered Writings of Bal-Makhshoves* (First Volume), S. Shreberk, Washington, DC, 1910.

5   Tina Lunson, translator, *Haynt*, Warsaw, August 31, 1919.

6   Sol Liptzin, *The Flowering of Yiddish*, Thomas Yoseloff: NY, 1963, pp. 76-87.

# ONE

Reb Berl, tax trustee, was a schoolteacher, a successful man about town. Ever since he'd been an official in the kosher meat tax office, none but the children of well-to-do families studied in his school.

"Reb Berl," the other teachers said with envy, "is a lucky man. Even though he doesn't study very carefully with his students, he's deemed an excellent teacher. And though he hits them, as we all do, and whips them, as is the custom, he's called a good, intelligent man, worthy of the most precious children."

And fortune smiled on him. It was an honor for a child to be taken into Reb Berl's cheder. And Reb Berl really understood how to beat his pupils and knew, further, how to deal with their fathers and mothers.

Leybele, the only son of Reb Shloyme, head of the tax office, could turn the whole schoolroom upside down, but Reb Berl never really saw or got very angry with him. He knew just how dear and precious Leybele was to his mother, Sheyndele, and how great an honor it was that he, Reb Berl, sometimes went back to her home with her husband to make a blessing after Shabbes services.

He told Sheyndele what a clever, quiet child her Leybele was in school—no evil eye—and he marveled that at first people were scared of him, saying Leybele was a prankster, a capricious boy, and that he would be hard to manage without a blow.

"I don't know," said Reb Berl wonderingly. "With me he is quiet as a little dove. He obeys, he learns, and wants to learn—no evil eye. And can Leybele say I hit him? That I even get angry with him? I truly can't understand at all why someone would hit a little child in school! Hitting makes no sense! People should have sense, and in teaching, I tell you, lies patient good sense."

With the same good sense, Reb Berl argued continually with Menashe Milner when he complained about his two sons who were already in Berl's third level, but were still unable to read correctly. "Of course," said Berl, explaining to Menashe his error, "the harder it is to make progress in reading, the easier it will be later, you'll see, to step ahead in Khumesh with Rashi. It's really common knowledge that the greatest scholars, the sharpest minds, can't read a word of Hebrew. What more evidence do you need than this: our own Rabbi, may he be healthy, is certainly a genius, a shrewd and brilliant man, and nevertheless, he still makes mistakes in his Hebrew. And what's the story do you think? Simply, that a great mind doesn't trouble itself with trivialities; there'd be no sense in that. I assure you it will be in Khumesh, in answering Rashi, that your children will first display the progress I make with them. They have ardent little heads!"

Itsi the Textile Seller's rascal, who got the nickname Mischievous Moyshele at home, was also quite a problem in cheder, and right now it seems he'd broken the Rebbe's patience. Reb Berl lifted the leather whip to show the little mischief-maker how to have good manners in the teacher's presence, but the whip seldom fell on Moyshele.

It always—"accidentally"—fell instead on Yosele, son of Khyene the sexton's wife. Yosele had the privilege of sitting at the edge of the table in cheder and of having Reb Berl for his teacher, although the Rebbe very often forgot to do any learning with him.

Yosele, a quiet, scrawny child, sometimes received the blow with indifference, as if he were already quite used to it. But sometimes he cried and squirmed. "You little fool," said the Rebbe to him in such cases, "why are you crying? I didn't mean it for you; I meant it for the mischief-maker. It's with him I have a complaint! And you, scamp," he said turning to Moyshele, "do you think that because I didn't get you this time you're home free? Tell him, Yosele, that the main point is not the blow but the intent, understand?"

Although Yosele didn't understand, just to hear a kind word from the Rebbe made him feel peaceful. But at other times, when Yosele sat hungry because his mother didn't have more than a piece of dry bread to send with him that day, or the Rebbe happened to be angry with the Rebbetzin for scolding him about this and that, or the rich men's precious children had worn out the Rebbe's patience, at such a moment the whip fell on Yosele's back with such force—accidentally it seemed—that the child gave out a heartrending cry, turned black and blue for a few seconds, and then sobbed quietly.

When this happened, the Rebbe let him cry it out, but if it continued for too long, he shouted, "Quiet! Not one more sound! Perhaps you're pampered at home with your mother, but here in school I hate privileged people. Nobody gets special treatment! Did I slaughter him? Maybe a flick on the back, accidentally, with the whip. Can't he be quiet?"

Once in a while, though seldom, it happened that Reb Berl became furious at all the children in cheder. Mischievously, one of the boys had broken a pane of glass, and Reb Berl knew he'd have to pay for it. "Twenty kopecks gone that can't be eaten or drunk," his wife, the Rebbetzin, screamed at him! She knew the guilty boy's mother would be very angry if anybody came asking for the price of the school's broken window. Or maybe it's something even worse: Mischievous Moyshele had shaken all the salt into the pot while the Rebbetzin's back was turned away for a moment. She tasted it, spit it out, and screamed: "Such a bunch of heretics! Spoiling the soup with salt so the Rebbe will have nothing to eat? Now you try it," she said, laying out a spoon for the Rebbe. "Won't you be proud of your lighthearted scholars!"

The Rebbe lifted the spoon to his mouth then quickly spit out the soup and shouted, "You'll all get beaten no matter who you are, blood will spurt!"

"Yosele!" he called to the poor child who sat in another room rocking the Rebbe's child. "Go in the yard near the dung heap. It seems to me a couple of old brooms are lying around. Choose a few good twigs and bring them in. You'll see how they'll spring on the skin."

Yosele's little heart told him that of all the boys, he'd be feeling the twigs first, but he was afraid not to go. He knew from experience that he'd prefer two lashes from the leather whip to one lash from the twigs, but he went out and brought them in.

The Rebbe took the twigs and brandished them in the air to inspire more dread in his young scholars. "So, what are you waiting for?" he asked Yosele, who was afraid to walk away to rock the child as he'd been doing before. "Unfasten your pants, I'll beat you first. And after that, everybody! Every last one!"

"Rebbe, I didn't do it. I was rocking the little one," Yosele tried to plead. "Ask the Rebbetzin. I never left the room!"

"It's all the same!" answered the Rebbe, making himself bold. "I didn't ask who actually did this and who didn't. If I'm going to beat every boy in the class, you're not better than the others. Quickly, don't beg. It'll go better for you!"

Yosele knew crying wouldn't help. He brought his hands from behind his back and began to loosen his pants. The patched and snagged trousers with no buttons, tied up here and there so they wouldn't fall off his tiny body, were not easily loosened. The Rebbe called out, "Whoever helps let down his trousers will get five fewer lashes."

A couple of boys lunged forward to help unbind the knotted trousers. Yosele remained like a stone, half-naked.

"Lie down!" the Rebbe commanded.

Yosele lay down and tears poured over the bench. The Rebbe pulled the shirt higher and saw the whole little body mottled and beaten. On the boy's back were the signs of last night's whipping: blue swollen stripes.

"Did your mother or father beat you today, poor thing?" the Rebbe asked suddenly.

"My mother didn't hit me; my father either," answered Yosele.

"Liar! Here are the signs, your skin's been stripped with a rope!" cried Reb Berl with his hand on the swollen stripes.

"Oy, Rebbe, it's been hurting me there since last night. It was your leather whip!" cried Yosele.

"A lie! A false accusation!" screamed Reb Berl. "When do I hit unless it happens to be a mistake—an accident?"

"Accident?" asked the poor child, but it was of no use.

"From an accident there would be no such signs," explained the Rebbe. "You're just trying to falsely accuse me! I do indeed give a whipping for false accusations. Remember children, whoever falsely accuses me of beating them will be beaten. And whoever holds the slanderer by the feet will today be exempt from a lashing!" All the boys jumped for the mitzvah.

The Rebbe counted the lashes: "One, two, three! This is how one strikes a boy who breaks a window mischievously! Four, five, six! A boy who pours salt into the Rebbe's dinner! Seven, eight, nine! And even harder do I smite the false accuser for lying, saying that I hit, that I raise welts on his skin! Remember this, children, for a slanderer I flay the skin off!"

Yosele cried, quivered, and bit the bench in pain until the Rebbe released him. Yosele's lips burned. His whole little face was wet and smeared with tears. He quickly pulled up his pants and tried hard to stop crying, but his little heart heaved and sobbed.

"Wash off your face and come study!" ordered the Rebbe. Yosele wiped his face with his sleeve. The Rebbe was not pleased and sent him to the kitchen to wash himself well. Before Yosele washed himself, he grabbed the water dipper and drank thirstily. His little heart burned and his tongue was dry from crying.

Later the Rebbe called out, "Speak!" and Yosele recited the Khumesh with all the correct translations and commentary. Another sob tore its way out of him. Reb Berl listened and calmed the child completely.

"That's the way, that's a completely different story!" said the Rebbe, exactly as if nothing had happened. "You see, now he recites Khumesh, it's a pleasure to hear, but sometimes one must smite. You understand, rascals?" he shouted at the other children. "One must smite so you don't become wild and break windowpanes or pour salt and spoil a dinner so the Rebbe has nothing to eat! Don't think you'll get off easy again. I'll strip off your skin! Now go eat dinner."

"Why aren't you going?" the Rebbe, now completely pleasant, asked Yosele.

"Today my mother didn't cook any dinner," answered Yosele, and from his little heart came a soft sigh like a delayed echo of his earlier crying.

"That's very good!" said the Rebbetzin as she handed the child to Yosele and ran out to grab something in the shop for her husband to eat. "You can hold the baby until I come back!"

# Two

Yosele was the first son born to Khyene the sexton's wife after she had already given birth to five little girls. Three of them, evidently the cleverest, soon realized that nobody rejoiced for their being here, not the father and mother, not the whole world. They quietly carried themselves back to their Maker, each with a different pretext: one from croup, the second from a bad case of the measles. The third came up with a bright idea and overturned onto herself a pot of boiling water; after she had cried absolutely enough for a day and a night, she bequeathed her share of the inheritance to the other two surviving sisters and stopped crying forever.

Khyene, who had never rejoiced of their lives, had nevertheless cried bitterly and lamented their deaths without consolation until God saw her grief and sent her a sixth child, a boy, and that was Yosele. "I have no more complaints for you, God in Heaven," Khyene said at Yosele's bris. "With one hand you punish the sinful mortal, with the other you console him. Probably you know, loving God, that one son is as dear to a mother as three daughters. I begged you for a son. You've taken from me three half-grown daughters, children bright as the sun, and you've given me a little boy. I thank You, loving God. You're right; Your judgment is right! Give the child long life and let his mother bring him up to the Torah, to the chuppah, and to good deeds."

And how great was Khyene's celebration when Yosele began to walk before he was one year old! Khyene taught him the blessing for food which is neither wine nor bread when he had barely begun to speak the words "papa" and "mama." From that day forward, Yosele did not even seek her breast without making the blessing.

At the age of two, Yosele already knew how to recite the *Moydeh Ani.* At three he knew the whole alphabet, complete with vowels. When he was five, Khyene had nothing more to teach her dear child. He had long since learned it all, and she began planning to send him to a good Rebbe's cheder. But it transpired, as it is said, "Man proposes and God disposes."

It was precisely then that a great misfortune befell her. Running about one winter evening gathering people for a meeting in the *besmedresh*—the study house—where he was sexton, her husband became chilled and suffered a lung inflammation. God had compassion and did not leave her son without a father. He survived, but he lost his position as sexton because he remained a sickly, broken man who coughed his soul out the whole day long.

Jews are not without compassion. The whole town was not without fairness. He was paid five guldens a week; however, a sexton's main revenue is the additional fees he receives: a wedding, a bris, a yortzeit. These, the new sexton took.

Then God in Heaven remembered to pay back an old debt to Khyene, and in such bitter times, he sent her to childbed with two boys, twins, to show her, probably, that she had made a mistake when she suspected God of sending her one son in the place of the three daughters He had taken. Here, she had three for three and should not complain! Although, actually, never since Yosele had been born had Khyene asked God to pay His debt to her, and she had made no complaint, but one must accept God's bounty. She somehow made two brisses in one day and began to raise the children.

In such a bitter situation, she couldn't even think of paying a teacher for Yosele's education. So when her husband Borekh was barely up out of his bed, she gave him the honor of teaching their son. "It's already time," she told her husband. "He's six years old."

Even when Borekh was healthy, he had been an angry, dry man, a stickler who had therefore never known how to create a following for himself as other sextons did. Especially now that he was an invalid, half-starving and with a merciless cough, he didn't spare his own child. In punishment of any triviality, he would let out the frustration of his bitter heart.

Khyene could not be quiet. Before every blow he gave Yosele, she sent out a curse: "May the hand of a father who gives his own son such a blow dry up! May God strike you, because you strike the forlorn child exactly as if he were, God forbid, a bastard."

But the more Khyene swore, all the more did the sickly father torture and batter the child. And no cantor on the most solemn occasion ever shed so many tears as the poor child shed every time he prayed in front of his father.

"Tell me, I beg you," Khyene once asked her husband in a kindly manner, "why do you flog him so?"

"Because he's a peasant, a fat head, an Esau!" Borekh answered in an equally pleasant way.

"With such peasant children and fat heads may God bless all Jewish mothers!" whispered Khyene.

"And perhaps in your eyes this one's not a fat head?" asked the father. "Exactly ten times I've told him the correct interpretation of this rabbinic decree and he still errs!"

"He still errs!" mimicked Khyene. "I believe the Omniscient One himself wouldn't understand it; it's of no substance. He'll understand your nonsense within a year."

"Go ahead, mock me, Khyene, as a goy mocks a Yiddish word. You should be ashamed! Feh, a disgrace, as I am a Jew! Wife, the rule is really stated as I specify. Look in the book of Jewish laws, the *Shulkhan Arukh!*"

"But why would one teach a child such complicated laws which he can't yet comprehend?" asked Khyene.

"This is why I say he's a peasant!" he answered.

"And do all boys his age understand this law?" she asked.

"Why do you compare our Yosele to other boys?" asked the sexton. "He could already be their teacher, do you understand? Nothing is too difficult for him, because he is a fine boy, and you yourself yearned for him to be a scholar of distinction. That's why he must be flogged. The Holy Torah does not fly into the head by itself; it must be driven in with beatings. I was beaten myself, probably more than I beat Yosele. And I wish you'd realize that I'm sure some day Yosele will say, 'Healthy be my father's hand which beat me. Consequently, I really understand!'"

The hope that Yosele would some day be a distinguished Talmudist and scholar as Borekh himself said, gave her the strength to stand by and watch, even though with pain in her heart and tears in her eyes, as her husband hurt her dear child, called him to repeat the same passage ten times over and over, and pinched him and punched him until he guessed what his father wanted.

Thus did Khyene, along with her child, finally reach the full measure of misery and pain. And finally, when she had torn her grateful son from her husband's hand, she swore that as long as she lived, as long as her eyes were open, she would never again allow the crazy father to teach their child.

"I'd be worse than you," she shrieked with a grieving heart, "if I let you continue to cool your sick heart on this unfortunate little soul!"

Noticing the swollen wounds on Yosele's skin, she shouted, "I'm a bandit, a cutthroat from the forest! No Jewish daughter would have so little heart as to hurt her own child! Oy, Master of the Universe, why did you write in your Holy Torah, 'As a father has mercy on his sons?' Here is a father, and here, look at his compassion!"

# THREE

A week passed and then another week, and Yosele wasn't studying. It was just Passover-time and Khyene consoled herself: "All the boys are free now, why should my Yosele be worse than the others? Let him rest up a little, let the blue marks from his father's beatings subside a bit, and meanwhile perhaps the Master of the Universe will show me a way my child can study the Holy Torah."

But Passover was barely over when all the boys began to go back to school. Khyene's worry and sadness intensified and kept her from sleeping at night. "My mind is so uneasy!" she said once with a heavy sigh and grabbed her head.

"What is it?" her husband asked. "Have your ships sunk in the ocean?"

"Someone who's got ships on the ocean worries about sinking ships," Khyene answered. "And someone who has a child worries about who will make him a Jew and teach him God's Holy Torah. And my worry perhaps is: what shall I do with our son Yosele, and where shall I get tuition? And my worry is greater than somebody worrying about their ships on the ocean."

"Let him go to the Talmud-Torah, the poor boys' school. It's the way all poor children study," was Borekh's advice.

"The poor boys' school? And so says his own father?" Khyene asked with a pained tone. "He'll be ruined! He'll get an insect infestation. He'll forget what he used to know. I know what those children come to. There's more than one poor mother who cries and laments because she sent her child, her orphan, to the poor boys' school. No, as long as I live and have strength, even if I have to plow the earth with my nose, my Yosele will not study in Talmud-Torah."

"Then give him away to a shoemaker," Borekh continued, not because he really meant it, but just to make his wife eat her heart out.

"It would be better you shouldn't live to see that," Khyene swore.

"Useless curses!" said Reb Borekh in spite. "What, a cobbler isn't a Jew?"

"Why aren't you a cobbler?" asked Khyene.

"I'd thank God if I were a cobbler," he retorted. "Perhaps I'd be healthy to this day, and we wouldn't lack bread as we do now."

"If only, Master of the Universe!" wished Khyene, mocking him. "If you were a cobbler, I wouldn't have become your wife. Maybe I'd have a husband now no worse than any other, and my children would have a father who would provide for them and not let their mother's head wither and thirst for her child's tuition!"

She began again after she'd cried herself out a bit. "You're a foolish man! I suppose you think it was your sallow face that so charmed my father, may he intercede for us, that he accepted you as his son-in-law? What was special about you was that you could study. It was your Torah knowledge that charmed me, and I let myself reason this way, 'Rather than be wife to a boor, to a coarse young man, even a rich one, I'll have a poor man, but a proper and fine Jew, a scholar.' And may God not punish me for my words, but even to this day, I hate a simple man, an ignoramus. I don't envy his wife's pearls or her good life with him.

"The other day I was at the cemetery for Khatskl Eisenkremer's funeral. I thought, 'I'd bury myself alive if I saw my son, like

Khatskl's son, a young man of sixteen or seventeen years, unable to say Kaddish even from the prayer book.' Sorele, his mother, stood with a river of tears flowing, and I asked myself, 'Why is Sorele crying? Does she cry for her husband, her breadwinner, who has just been laid in the ground? Or does she cry for her living disgrace: that her only son cannot even say Kaddish from the prayer book?'

"In the midst of it all, my heart said, 'Master of the Universe, rather than let a son of mine grow up to be such a boor like that one, unable to even say Kaddish for his mother and father, it would be better to bury him young!'"

"Look, I assure you, Yosele will be able to say Kaddish for you," Reb Borekh mocked his wife.

"Why not for you?"

"Let him say Kaddish for me, too!"

"Just to spite you, Yosele will be able to read a chapter of Mishnah and a page of Gemara," Khyene confidently goaded her husband.

Borekh, in a gathering rage, spit and answered, "I don't give a whiff of tobacco for your chapter of Mishnah and page of Gemara! She thinks the Gemara is everything. I swear, Yoyne the Water Carrier, although he doesn't even know how the Mishnah opens, earns a greater mitzvah than the Rabbi's Reb Arye, who sits all day in the warm, bright study house and studies Mishnah and Gemara! Sometimes, when you're away from the house all day, Yoyne the Water Carrier brings me a pail of water so the children and I won't die of thirst."

"You foolish Jew!" Khyene called out to him. "How is it you don't understand why Yoyne the Water Carrier sometimes brings you free water! Thanks to your poverty? Thanks to your illness, do you think? Is there a shortage of poor, sick people in our town? Will Yoyne bring free water to all of them? How would he support his wife and children? It's that Yoyne thinks, 'Reb Borekh the Sexton is a scholar, penniless and ill, poor thing,' and he earns a mitzvah by helping a scholar. But if you were a shoemaker or even a tailor you could die from thirst. You wouldn't find anybody who'd bring you a spoonful of water. Now do you see how valuable it is to be a scholar?"

"I don't give a whiff of tobacco for that!" hollered Reb Borekh, not because he really believed her, but because he had a special anger towards the Rabbi's Reb Arye who was always his adversary. "Not a whiff of tobacco, as I'm a Jew, for Reb Arye's erudition and Torah!" He barely had breath enough to repeat this before he was gasping and coughing.

Khyene brought him a little water and held his head so he wouldn't fall off the bench from coughing. "You see," she said with compassion, "God has already paid you for your sinful talk. See, it doesn't matter to me at all that my Yosele be a Jew like the Rabbi's Reb Arye who lacks high-mindedness and honor! No matter," she suddenly said courageously, "I've been a fool, worrying my head so! 'To the degree that you help yourself, God also helps you.' God willing, tomorrow I'll give Yosele to a teacher. The Master of the Universe will have to send the tuition!"

# Four

From the rich wives she often visited, Khyene had often heard that Berl the Trustee was a dear, clever teacher who knew how to treat children and that his students really made progress with him. Thus she decided to enroll Yosele in his cheder, even though she knew he was not an inexpensive choice. She also knew that "To the degree you help yourself, God also helps you." Hoping that He would help by providing a couple of rubles each term, she took Yosele with her to meet Reb Berl.

Berl looked at her with wonder as she declared that she wanted her son to be enrolled, and he answered that he already had a full enrollment and could not take on any more boys. "What do you mean, you've already filled your school?" Khyene complained. "Where is it written that a teacher can have nine students and a tenth is forbidden?"

"I can't, as I'm a Jew, I simply cannot!" Reb Berl swore.

"Why?"

"Go explain something to a woman!" Reb Berl grumbled.

"Reb Berl! First God, afterwards you. The child is my whole life," Khyene began heatedly. "Half a life he cost me, the other half I'm ready to give for him, every minute, and I don't intend, dear God, that my son should study for free. It's not as though you and I were related. I understand you have to make a living. I tell you, your tuition will be brought to you at school every first of the month, with thanks. Maybe you're afraid because I'm a poor woman and you wonder how I'll get the money? I tell you: God, who feeds me and gives me the strength to slave for my sick husband and all my miserable children, will give me strength to struggle even harder to find the rubles for my child's tuition. And what am I asking of Him? Tuition for the Rebbe who teaches my son the Holy Torah! Master of the Universe! Can you really have the heart to deny my pious desire? I'll pay you, Reb Berl, as much as all your well-to-do housewives pay."

"Does your son know anything yet?" Reb Berl asked, thinking to get from her the confession that her son really knew nothing, so that a lesser teacher would be sufficient for him.

"Listen to him and see for yourself what a clever boy he is. It will be a delight for you to teach him!"

Berl interrogated Yosele and marveled at how much the boy knew and how well he remembered what he had learned. Yosele already knew more than all his other students. He gave Yosele a pat on the head and said: "A fine boy, a very fine boy. A pity, honestly, a pity!"

Hearing Reb Berl praise her child, Khyene felt tears in her eyes. "How do you answer me now, Reb Berl?"

"You know what I'll say to you?" said Reb Berl after a few minutes of thought. "I really pity you. Naturally, I would not be asking for your rubles for my tuition, except what would my wife say? And you also have to remember, she knows that without money the peasant doesn't give potatoes nor a little wagon-full of wood, and the shopkeeper gives no bread and no barley. One must pay rent, you understand? So get it in your head, my ten rubles a semester must be paid. Your son, understand me, must be taught differently; the rich boys aren't as advanced as he; whatever I teach them is enough, but one must spend a lot of time teaching one as special as your son!"

But Reb Berl remained reluctant. "One more thing stands

in my way," he said. "Will the fathers and mothers of my other students agree to have your son study in the same class with their children?"

"Why wouldn't they allow him in?" asked Khyene with fury. "Is my Yosele perhaps not as pious as their children? Was my father Reb Yosele the Preacher, may he have a happy Paradise, not such a pious and distinguished scholar that even our Rabbi himself used to consult with him? I swear to God that my child already has more learning in just one foot than your other students have in their heads!"

Berl understood and he wasn't going to argue with her, so he said sharply, "If you want me to take your child into my class, you must go to the wealthy households and win them over. You must convince the housewives so they won't complain later!"

It cost Khyene more than enough conversation, begging, and blessings before Sheyndele, the Taxman's wife, agreed to make no complaints. Khyene only had to promise her that Yosele would be clean and tidy, and Berl had to promise to pay attention so that Yosele would not get too friendly with her Leybele, or cheat Leybele out of his lunch or one kopeck of the cash she gave him each day to take to school.

Once Sheyndele made this agreement, the mothers of Berl's other students said the same, and one fine morning, Khyene washed her child, dressed him in a new jacket for which she had paid ten whole gulden on the previous day, and told him that from then on he must wake up earlier each day and go to Reb Berl's school.

"See, my child," she told him with tears in her eyes, "I have delivered you from your father's hand, which would have killed you or left you a cripple if I had let you study with him any longer. I'm doing a lot more for you now than my strength allows. I've obligated myself to pay ten rubles a semester and my head is worrying away about where to earn the ten rubles! I won't eat or sleep, my child, so that I don't come up short when it comes to your studies! See to it, my child, my crown, that you want to study! This is my only consolation in this world and my entire comfort in the next.

"You can't look to your father, the invalid, poor thing, nor to me, even though I'm driven to forget my pains and provide you all with food. Can you just wait, so I can do more good things for you and brighten your dark world? The only consolation and salvation for a poor child is the Holy Torah, which God, blessed be He, has given His people *Yisroel!*

"If you study Torah and understand it, it will lift you from your mother's poverty. You'll become a fine lad, and when the lucky hour comes, you'll find a wealthy man who'll want you as a bridegroom for his daughter. He'll give you a big dowry, and for love of you, he'll bring your father and mother good fortune. Even your poor sisters' luck will, thanks to you, begin to shine. Your mother's misery will be laid aside, and who will be my equal?

"Meanwhile, Yosele, you must have only one thing in mind: to want to study and to succeed in your learning! Remember not to be too friendly with the schoolboys; don't envy their fine clothes, or their good things, or the money you'll see they have. Their fathers and mothers are rich and can give them plenty of good things to take to school; your father and mother are poor folk. But you have more sense than they, and if you'll just study, after a while you'll be richer, too. Remember, Yosele, what I tell you. Promise you'll obey!"

Khyene said all this with tears. Seeing her, Yosele cried as well. As they both wiped the tears away, Khyene took Yosele to Reb Berl's school.

# FIVE

In the beginning, Reb Berl treated Yosele like his other students. He'd stand him in front of the other boys as an example, to show them how one should obey a Rebbe and how one needs to remember what one learns. However, the Rebbetzin began to order Yosele around, treating him as a poor child, her husband's charity case enrolled out of pity. Sometimes she sent him to the corner store for salt and barley groats, or into the other room to rock her little Khayele when she had no time to sit by the cradle. Gradually she became so used to this, she used to complain to her husband that he occasionally kept Yosele too long at the Khumesh when there wasn't a bit of wood in the house with which to cook dinner.

Little by little Reb Berl himself began to look away from Yosele, to forget to study with him, and sometimes, when he was angry at Leybele, the son of Sheyndele the Taxman's wife, and grabbed up his leather whip to "honor" him with it, the Rebbe would think, "This is Leybele, Sheyndele's precious, indulged little child. With this blow I will lose favor with Sheyndele."

So his hand would come down slowly on Yosele. He quickly excused himself, it was Leybele he'd meant to deal with.

Yosele himself also understood that this blow fell to him by mistake, particularly because Berl dealt it with pity and it didn't hurt much; he didn't cry or complain. But the mistakes started to come more frequently, and from one time to the next, harder and harder. Yosele tried crying, shouting, being completely silent, and sobbing quietly. It was all in vain!

Reb Berl became so used to making these mistakes, as if Yosele had been created from the beginning to receive them, that his leather whip always "accidentally" fell upon Yosele, no matter whom it had been aimed at. The poor child knew he was not guilty, that he had not earned the lash, but he did not understand that the Rebbe was guilty. First, because the Rebbe himself said it was accidental; second, because he was used to being beaten at home. He almost never knew why his father hit him; he only knew that when it hurt he cried out, shouted, and sobbed, even though he didn't want to shout or sob. But in the last few days he felt things were getting worse.

It had been two months already and Khyene had not earned an extra kopeck to send to the Rebbe for his pay. Reb Berl had already given it up for lost and figured he was teaching Yosele for free. "And why should I teach for free?" he used to ask himself as he put all his anger at Khyene for doing the injustice of not paying him into the whip and the rod.

"I told her earlier that I cannot teach her son for free!" he thought. "Yosele will tell this to his mother and she will understand that the Rebbe is angry. She'd better pay me! It wasn't I who begged to bring her child into my school. She wouldn't let up and I took him in, so she should pay me. If not, then to hell with him. At least I won't have to worry about him giving my little rascals a smack in return when they batter him. He's a quiet boy and doesn't annoy anyone; but these rascals even wear out my patience. And he's not more than a child. One day he might hit one of them, leaving a bruise. And that's all I need! I get it from all sides. I've already been hearing from Sheyndele about the favor she did me, allowing me to take a poor child into my school!"

With such words, Reb Berl used to justify hurting the poor child, letting his wife boss him around like an unpaid servant, and too often allowing his other students—with their full bellies—to hit the half-hungry Yosele, just because he was poorer than they!

Yosele had, however, not told his mother anything about what was happening in cheder. First, it's forbidden to tell tales from school; second, he had such pity on his forlorn mother that, seeing her cry, he too had to cry, his own pain and misery forgotten.

"Why did God create the poor man in the world?" he often heard his mother complaining when he came home from school. "Why give the poor man children to suffer troubles and pain, to be hungry and cold, if He doesn't give anything to nourish and maintain them, or to dress their nakedness so they, poor things, will not perish from the cold? 'Eat, Mama, eat!' they beg their hungry mothers. But what will you eat, dear children? 'Here, eat my flesh, the skin off my bones. I won't feel a greater pain than that I have so little to give you!'"

Observing Yosele coming home faint from school, she asks, "What can I give the poor child? From eight in the morning until nine at night he sits, thirsty and hungry, poor thing. Now he comes home to his mother to break his unsought fast, and his wretched mother hasn't even earned a bit of bread today, although she's run for miles from one rich person to another. For once, God should see your desolation and my grief, my poor child! There's no dinner today. Lie down and sleep, Yosele, you poor, hungry baby!"

And then she cried so hard he forgot his hunger and, crying, too, answered her, "Mama, I don't want to eat, I don't want to eat. Don't cry, don't cry, Mama!"

Another time he found his mother as she sat hunched over the cradle where his two little brothers, the twins, both lay sick unto death, poor things. She wrung her hands, big round tears trickling one after another down her sunken cheeks as she complained, "My poor babies! Why did I bring you into the world? What did I have against your pure little souls? Your little lips are burning, cracked from thirst. Your little bones are withering away. A hellish fire burns in your skin and eats you like a light! Oh, an iron heart must yield and melt looking at you. And how can a mama's heart, seeing this, not break apart, my guiltless little souls!"

And the unhappy mother began to tear the hair from her head in misery. Yosele also cried himself to pieces, but the mother, not feeling like herself, screamed at him, "I needed you like a hole in the head! You think I have few troubles besides you? There's food here, eat up and go to sleep!"

But Yosele cried even more until finally Khyene unleashed her heart's woe on him. She hit him, pinched him, yet she herself did not know why. Yosele let her hit and pinch him. He kissed his mother's hand, and it seemed to him that this was good for her. He also felt his own heart, convulsed with compassion, becoming more peaceful. When his mother stopped crying, he lay down to sleep with no hope that tomorrow would be any happier or better than today.

# Six

Once, going home hungry and depressed from school, Yosele picked something up in the street. He felt there was some money in it and ran home breathlessly. Sweaty and tired from running, he could barely be heard: "Mama, see what I found!"

Khyene took it. It was a pocketbook with a few rubles. She quickly closed the door so no outsider could enter, and looked through this marvelous find—a right bit of silver and two paper bills, about twelve rubles in all.

"God sent this at the right time!" Khyene happily exclaimed. Borekh, her sick husband, dragged himself up off the bench to have a look at what Yosele had found.

"Perhaps the owner hasn't yet had a chance to announce his loss. Don't rejoice yet!" Borekh said, seeing her celebrate.

"Who cares what you say!" she answered, "The Master of the Universe sent Yosele this miracle so I'd have something to pay his school bill with."

"Where did you find this?" Borekh asked Yosele.

"In the street near Khaym the Saloonkeeper's place!"

"In the street, in a public place near the saloon, and today is a market day; then it might be a legitimate godsend," Borekh said. "Therefore, Khyene," he said, "in all fairness, you should go tomorrow and buy me a new pair of shoes. I don't have any even for walking around in the house."

"Buying you shoes will have to wait," Khyene answered. "First of all, I'll take four rubles and send them with Yosele for the Rebbe. And if shoes are going to be bought, I'll buy Yosele a new pair; he has to go to school and it tears my heart out seeing how his little toes peek out through his shoes. Why should my child be shamed? After all, he studies in a rich boys' school. After that, at the market tomorrow, I'll buy a few potatoes, firewood, a couple pounds of cornmeal so there can at least be bread in the house. And if there's anything left after that, before I buy you shoes, I'll buy myself a pair. After all, you sit in the house, but I must run around earning a kopeck."

"You and your rebellious son!" Borekh grumbled to himself. "So I need nothing, nothing! Give the Rebbe two rubles, that will be enough, and with a ruble buy me a pair of shoes!"

"How can I get through to you?" Khyene couldn't restrain herself. "Don't you see that God sent this, perhaps all of it, for school tuition? 'To the measure that people take care of things, to that measure will God help them.' I committed myself to paying for my child's schooling, and now God has really sent the Rebbe's fee straight into Yosele's hand. Perhaps this is a test from the Master of the Universe. He wants to see how I fulfill the solemn oath I swore to Reb Berl to pay him!"

The next morning, Khyene twisted a three-ruble note and one silver ruble into a paper and bundled it into Yosele's fringed vest. "Give this to the Rebbe," she said, "and don't tell anyone any tales about where you found it." She then ran to the market to buy things for the house.

Yosele gave the money to the Rebbe, and the Rebbe gave him a pat and said he was quite a fine boy! He studied with him and gave him not a single blow, not one smite accidentally or on purpose. Too, the Rebbetzin didn't order him around and actually went to the store herself, and he only rocked the child for a couple of minutes, and the Rebbetzin said, "Long life to you, Yosele. What a good child you are. I truly love you!"

Also, at lunchtime he went home to eat just like all the other boys, because in the morning his mother had told him to come home for food. She cooked lunch today, although she'd given him a few coins to buy a little something at school if his little heart was fainting from hunger. And how good his father was to him today!

Khyene managed their find cleverly: for twelve gulden she bought a pair of women's shoes for herself and a pair of warm slippers for her husband. "Pity on him as well!" she said, and there was a very good dinner, dairy farfel, which Yosele really loved.

The next day and the day after were the same. His mother bought him a new pair of shoes, and she herself sewed him a new pair of pants. Their neighbor, a tailor, had cut them for her in exchange for a good word. And also the Rebbe was good. The four rubles had convinced him to lay aside the leather whip and make no more "mistakes."

Even in cheder, everything was completely different. Since the Rebbe was good, his students weren't bad. Yosele wasn't hungry any more. And when he arrived home, things were better: his mother wasn't crying and his father wasn't cursing. His father even seemed to cough less.

And this went on for a couple of weeks. Yosele almost forgot his previous troubles and thought himself the equal of all his schoolmates. But how frightened and downhearted he was on the day that his mother again sent him to cheder with nothing for the whole day but a piece of dry bread! He got angry and wanted to fuss about it, but when he saw the tears in his mother's eyes, he headed off to school with what she gave him, and little by little, the previous pain and troubles returned.

The Rebbetzin commanded him not only to go to the store and rock her baby, but also gave him the honor of going with her to the river to drag the laundry. Each day the Rebbe made mistakes with his whip, and although this didn't hurt Yosele any more now than it did before, still it hurt his little heart every time, and he began to feel the pain longer and deeper than before. Before, he hadn't asked any questions or had complaints about the beatings he received; he'd only known one thing: that a smiting hurts, that hunger is painful. Now, however, he sensed, although not clearly, that beyond blows and hunger there is something that hurts even more: poverty and the injustices done to him because of his poverty.

He didn't speak about it. He didn't even think it through, but in his little heart he felt that his mother's poverty alone was to blame for all his misery, and he began to wish he was rich, like Leybele, Moyshele, and all the other boys in cheder. And when he prayed, he didn't listen to the words as he used to. Instead, his little heart begged, "God, let me find a purse full of money again. A lot of money, so my mother will be as rich as Leybele's mother, like Moyshele's mother, so she won't cry, and father won't cough and curse, and the Rebbe won't beat me!"

He lost himself in such thoughts and sometimes didn't know what the Rebbe asked when they studied. He didn't hear the Rebbetzin call, and caught some blows for not answering instantly when the Rebbetzin shouted for him. Often his distracted daydreaming caused Reb Berl to mock him and flick his nose.

Reb Berl also told the other children to flick Yosele's nose if they caught him distracted and dreaming. The kids didn't need to hear any more than that; Yosele's nose was always red and swollen because of his thoughts, which nobody knew.

Going from home to school and back again, he kept his head down, his little eyes seeking the windfall he begged for three times a day in all his prayers—the windfall that God might send him.

Also, in his sleep, he dreamed he was standing in shul. Everyone was praying. And he was praying, too, begging God that his mother might become rich, his father might not cough, that he might be equal to the other boys in school, and that the Rebbe might no longer whip him or flick his nose.

He often dreamed that he found money. Here lies a coin; he picks it up and wants to run to his mother, but he sees another in the sand, and another, a lot of coins. He already has full hands, full pockets, but before he has time to gather it all up, his father coughs and he awakens. It was a dream. He himself doesn't believe it. He feels around in his bed, no coins, nothing.

Another time he dreamt he found money, a lot of money, but from the start he didn't believe it. Was it true or just a dream like the previous time—like all the previous times? He tried proofs to determine whether it was true, and it seemed this time it really was true: he saw his mother in the kitchen, he heard his father coughing, he heard his brothers crying in the cradle. This time he was certain it was not a dream. But then there was a shift. He began to dream something totally different: the school, the Rebbe, the Rebbetzin, and the laundry by the river. He forgot the money entirely. Suddenly he remembered he had found money, but where? When he awoke, he felt his heart so heavy, so weak.

Khyene noticed her Yosele becoming a different child. Something was distracting him. He was heavyhearted and spoke less than he used to.

"What's the matter, my child, does your head hurt?" she asked. She laid her hand on Yosele's forehead to see if it was hot.

"Or perhaps your stomach, Yosele?" she asked, terrified, looking into his despairing eyes.

"Nothing hurts, mother," Yosele answered.

"Then why are you so downhearted and never cheerful?"

"Mama," Yosele replied, "when will you be rich like Leybele's mother?"

"When God wills it, dear child. You want your mother to be rich?"

"I want it, Mama. I pray to God that you'll be rich!"

"Why do you want this so much?" she asked.

"If you were rich, you would never cry. You wouldn't fight with father, father wouldn't cough, and he wouldn't swear at me." But he was afraid to say, "And the Rebbe wouldn't hit me."

"God may answer us," Khyene called out piously, raising her eyes to Heaven. Don't worry, Yosele. The very God who already sent you one windfall will send you another, an even greater one!" Khyene had not found any other possible way to become rich.

"Don't despair, Yosele," she consoled him further, "God has many more wealthy people, and the wealthy people can lose a lot more money for you to find and to make your mother happy and yourself even more so!"

A few weeks went by this way. In vain he prayed to God, in vain his little head bent to the ground, in vain his eyes searched. But it was like his dream: when he stood up, his hands were empty.

Meanwhile he wanted to eat. Meanwhile his father coughed and swore and shouted, "Peasant, Esau! You're a burden on your mother, like death! Are you too sick to go out and earn like all the other poor children?" But Yosele didn't know how to earn.

His mother, he saw, was also always depressed, black as the earth. She'd also been starting, little by little, to cough, and she often grabbed at her heart.

It was no better in school. There, in addition to the blows and nose-pinches, he'd gotten a nickname: "The Egghead!" He didn't know what it meant, but even the Rebbe called him nothing else. And he wanted to be rich even more than he did before.

One day, Sheyndele sent her servant to school with a whole kerchief-full of silver coins. "The mistress has sent you six rubles!" said the servant and then left.

The Rebbe began to gather up the coins. At that very moment he saw, through the window, that his landlord, Pinkhes the Cabinetmaker, was coming to see him. With both hands he grabbed the money and shook it into his pockets. A few coins fell while he was grabbing for them and rolled down to the ground, and a few fell into Yosele's lap.

A couple of the boys wanted to crawl under the table to gather up the coins, but the Rebbe winked to indicate that nobody should move. Yosele was also afraid to give the Rebbe the money that had come falling towards him.

"Good morning, Reb Berl," Pinkhes said as he came in.

"Good morning to you," answered the Rebbe. "Have a seat, Reb Pinkhes!"

"I didn't come to sit," answered Pinkhes. "Let me come straight to the point and then leave. It's past time, Reb Berl. You owe me more than six rubles in rent. You've already let a year run by."

"Why should you run?" asked the Rebbe, "When I have it, I'll bring it to your house happily."

"So you're giving me the same answer now as you gave half a year ago? No, now you can't put me off again. This time you must give me what's mine!" Pinkhes said angrily.

"Well, but if I don't have it?" asked the Rebbe.

"What do you mean, you don't have it? Why is that my concern? Give me as much as you can. Give me three rubles, and I'll wait a month for the other three."

"Perhaps after Shabbes. Today I have nothing for you, Reb Pinkhes."

"I'm not going to believe you any more, Reb Berl. You always tell me you don't have it. I know perfectly well that your students' families have good money. I wish my tenants could pay so well!"

"Today I have literally nothing. On my word of honor, I have nothing! As you see me to be a Jew! Even if you were to slaughter me for a kopeck!" Reb Berl swore.

Yosele heard the Rebbe swear falsely. "May one swear falsely?" his little heart shrieked in him. His blood began to boil. He touched the few coins in his lap. Not knowing what he was doing, he hid them in his clothes.

Pinkhes left without any money. The clock struck one, and the Rebbe told his students to go eat lunch. Yosele ran home and with contrived gaiety cried out, "Mama, I found money again!"

Khyene became lighthearted. She believed God was literally doing a miracle for her. She'd been waiting a long time for her child to bring her glad tidings of a new windfall, this time a real treasure, a big treasure. God had shown her that Yosele was a lucky child and God helped her through him. So why not show her a second time? Had her child's luck become a complete, real prosperity?

But how downhearted she was to see that Yosele was holding out only two twenty-kopeck pieces and one ten-kopeck piece.

"That's all?" she asked. "That's not worthy of a celebration!"

Yosele, feeling guilty, was afraid to raise his eyes. He stood confused.

"Khyene, there's something wrong here!" his father interjected, "This is a fishy story. Why don't *I* find money, why don't *you* find money? You spend more time in the street than he does."

"What are you saying," Khyene asked, "He has better eyes than mine—he sees in an instant and I don't—and why shouldn't he be luckier than I?"

"Where did you find it?" Borekh half-asked, half-shrieked. Yosele stood silent.

"Why are you so quiet, you devil?" Borekh shouted with all his strength. "Where did you find the money?"

Yosele began to shiver as with a fever.

"I bet you, Khyene, he stole it," Borekh said, and coughed with anger.

"Better I should not have lived to see this, Master of the Universe!" Khyene shrieked, wringing her hands. "You found this, Yosele?" she tried to ask him, although her heart had already told her this was no simple situation.

"I found it!" Yosele quietly answered, shivering.

"Found it? You didn't find this! How does one find loose change in the street?" she asked, this time crying out with more suspicion.

Yosele didn't answer; he just began to cry quietly.

"May your name be blotted out!" his father shouted as he sprang up. "Let me at him, Khyene. I'll make a corpse of him! Where did you find this? Quickly, come; show me. If you don't, I'll beat you black and blue!"

Yosele cried but answered not a word.

"Where did you find it?" Khyene also shouted. "Speak up! Show me. Woe is me! You stay silent? You steal? What a blow to your desolate mother!"

With this, she threw herself at him like a wild woman, tearing, pinching, and biting him. "Oy, oy!" she shrieked, "it would have been better to bury you as a baby than to raise you to be a thief who'll blacken my name!

"Why is this happening to me, Master of the Universe? Did I not sacrifice enough for him? Have I not bloodied myself enough? Torn from myself the bites of bread, made for him a shirt, a shoe, a little garment? My child was to be a scholar; my child was to know how to study. I didn't ask more than that from you, Master of the Universe, and this is my consolation, the comfort I've lived to see?"

Tears poured from her eyes. She cried hysterically. Yosele had never seen her cry so wildly. He knew he was guilty. He had known from the first that what he was doing was wrong and he regretted it strongly. But how to correct it? He didn't know, and so he blurted out, "Mama, don't cry, I won't do it any more!"

"Tell us already, whose money is this?" Borekh shouted.

"It's the Rebbe's," Yosele confessed in tears.

"You see, mother dear," Borekh shouted at his wife. "Who knows him better, me or you? Let me at him, he won't be happy when I get through with him!" And he started in on the forlorn child.

"Borekh, you'll cripple him!" Khyene shrieked, and barely managed to tear the unlucky child from his father's hands.

"A thief is worse than a cripple!" he shouted. "A cripple is a punishment from God, not a disgrace, but a thief is a punishment *and* a disgrace, both in this world and the next. Compassion is cruelty! Show you're really a mother and set him straight. I have no more strength; the cough chokes me completely. Oy, he's bringing my death closer, a violent death to him!"

"My child is a thief, a thief? My world is dark and bitter!" the unhappy mother shrieked. "From whom did he learn this? Is your father a thief? Is your darkened mother a thief? Tell us! I'll bury you this very day. Who taught you to be a thief?"

"This is not the sort of thing one learns," Borekh explained after coughing. "It's born in you. It's in the blood, Heaven preserve us!"

"Born! In the blood? How did he come to have such blood?" Khyene interrupted, wringing her hands. "Are there, then, thieves in my family? He should be a Jew as holy and upright as my father was, rest in peace, and as my brothers are, they should have long lives. Perhaps it was from someone in *your* family that destined my child would become a thief!"

"He may resemble my family," Borekh called out, "but that's not what I meant at all. You are a woman, Khyene, and it's written in the Kaballah that a woman is never sure if her children resemble her or her husband's family. But as for bad blood: sometimes a bad encounter is to blame, sometimes an evil thought. It happens sometimes that something is overheard when foolish women talk endlessly, gossiping about thieves and rascals. And so the child is born with this blood, Heaven preserve us! Do you understand? That's my opinion."

"I understand, but it is small consolation," Khyene lamented. "No, no!" she suddenly began to shriek. "He will not remain a thief! A young sapling can be bent to and fro, and if this has come to him from a bad encounter, perhaps I can tear out, root out, suck out this bad blood! My child, Reb Yosele the Preacher's grandson, will not be a thief! Come, you little worm, come to your Rebbe. Give him back his money; he'll skin you alive. Let all the boys see. That will teach you! Perhaps you'll heal from the evil spirit that's gotten into you!"

And she grabs the hand of the child she has loved until now, and she runs as if some force is carrying her, not noticing at all that she is dragging behind her a weak, hungry, beaten, and whipped child who no longer has strength or breath enough to run behind her.

"God help you, dear Rebbe!" Khyene called out as she entered the cheder. She had to rest a few minutes to catch her breath.

"Oh, a conclusion?" Reb Berl guessed. "I thought he was too quiet in school. So he's the opposite at home, is that true, Yosele?"

"If only he hadn't learned this evil," Khyene answered with tears in her eyes. "He didn't learn this naughty behavior at home. That's why I'm lamenting so! He was always a good child, a quiet child. Suddenly a bad hour falls on him. He takes money and brings it home! 'Found money,' he said. He really thought he'd make a happy day for me. Woe! And I, a woman, what does a sinful female know? I really believed he'd found it. But my husband, shall he become healed from his illness, poor thing, understood from the first glance that this was not a legitimate windfall! So I've dragged Yosele here, torn half-dead from his father's hands, and from various blows and bites he got from me, may God grant me a lucky year! But why should I go on and on? The shoe has already dropped: he admitted this is your money. How did it come to him? I was so confused, I completely forgot to ask. Take it, Rebbe, I've brought it to you. I'd rather take poison than stolen money! My child will not be a thief!"

"Leah!" the Rebbe shouted to his wife, "See, one shouldn't be suspicious of a person. Here is the half-ruble that was missing from Sheyndele's six rubles! And you shouted that the servant himself stole it away, and he received blows from Reb Shloyme to make him confess. See who the thief is? Would you ever have thought it of him? Such a quiet worm to be such a blackguard!"

"Still water runs deep. I expect a sad end for him!" the Rebbetzin responded, raising Yosele's little chin with her hand.

"Speak up, you little thief, what else have you stolen that I don't know about?"

"Leah, don't take this wrong," Khyene spoke up. "Don't think such a thing! This situation is my punishment, my disgrace, but I swear to you, it's the first evil hour he's had, the first and the last. He's already been beaten enough by his father and me, and I've come to ask your husband, let his hands be healthy, that he should also punish Yosele severely so he may be a lesson to others, and to warn my child to be very careful and never let such evil hold him in its sway again." Khyene again cried bitterly.

"Don't cry, Khyene," the Rebbe consoled her, "I'm sure this was literally the first time Yosele committed such a foolish deed. I thank you for the half ruble you've brought back to me; it certainly takes me quite a lot of drudgery and toil to earn half a ruble. My only worry now is that because of this, I came to be suspicious of Sheyndele's servant. In good faith I tell you, I don't know how things should proceed. All that's lacking now is for Sheyndele to find out your son was the thief. She'll complain that I took such a boy into the cheder. I don't hold this against her, but she'll again ask me who is right: she or I? She always tells me, 'One should guard vigilantly against the poor, as one would against fire! Everything bad is in their children!' and I always swear it's not that way, that she's in error. On the other hand, justice should be done to the servant, whom I unfairly accused, and whom Reb Shloyme has meanwhile treated to some fiery blows.

"Here's what I think: I'll tell the servant lad that I've found the money. No story will be told to Sheyndele at all. I warn you youngsters, I'll strip the flesh off any of you who discloses what you've seen and heard here. Remember, rascals, what I say, and swear you'll disclose nothing!" All the boys promised not to tell.

"And now, Yosele, it's your turn," Reb Berl said. "Don't be afraid, Khyene. A great strength lies in the rods. And if he had a thought to become a thief and seek the taste of a bit of pilfering, he'll soon know how bitter and sour it is, and will spit it out. So, this will cure him!"

With these words, Reb Berl plucked a few sticks from a new broom, took Yosele by his little hands, loosened the boy's pants himself, and laid him down on the bench.

"Khyene, your mitzvah is to hold his feet!" the Rebbetzin said turning to Khyene. "That will show him that his mother herself really knows what's happening and wants him to be beaten for such a thing. God will see your grief and will save your child."

Khyene gathered all her strength in order to stand witness, but she barely glimpsed his skin, flayed by new and old blows and lashes, when a wave of pity grabbed her. Her head began to swim. It grew dark before her eyes, and she felt a swoon coming on.

The Rebbe didn't look at her. He beat Yosele as hard as he could. Suddenly, with her last strength, Khyene shrieked out, "With compassion, Rebbe, have pity!" and fainted.

# SEVEN

When Khyene came to, she used her apron to wipe her face with the cold water the Rebbetzin had spewed on her from her mouth, and saw Yosele standing near by, shrieking like a wild thing, "Mama, Mama, oy, Mama, don't die!"

Yosele had watched the Rebbe pressing on his mother's nose and seen the Rebbetzin take swig after swig of water in her mouth and spray it out on his mother's face. Still, she lay pale as a corpse, not moving or even making a groan. Yosele thought his mother was already dead, and his anguish caused him to forget his own agony and pain.

"Oy, Mama, don't die, don't die," he shrieked and kissed his mother's moist, cold hands. "Dear mother, I will never, never steal again!"

"You're alive, Yosele?" Khyene asked in a faint voice. "You are standing on your own little legs, my poor child?"

"What are you saying, Khyene, God be with you!" the Rebbetzin shouted out indignantly. "What did you think, that my husband's such a brigand he would beat your child to death, Heaven forbid? Doesn't your boy deserve, in fact, even stronger blows? He was merely beaten as all children are beaten, even those more delicate than he."

"I speak, but do I know what I am saying?" Khyene apologized. "My pain speaks in me. No such trial should come to any Jewish mother, such woe, such misery. Don't be angry, Reb Berl! Your hands should be healthy! And if your rods are a medicine for him, and if he never again does such a thing, then I'll pray for you my whole life long and never forget your kindness."

Khyene's throat was dry. "Yosele, give me a little water," she asked, and as she took a swallow, she felt a bit stronger and turned again to her child, "See what you've made of your mother? One more moment and I would perhaps never have opened my eyes again. The good people have done a mercy not for me, but for you and your sick father and my poor children, by not letting me die before my time.

"Speak up, Yosele. If you want me to keep living so you and your sisters and little brothers won't have to be wandering, desolate little orphans from this day forward, you must never do such a foolish thing again, such a heavy sin and disgrace as thievery! Remember, you must not covet another's goods; you must abhor another's money as Jews avoid pigs. Avoid anything owned by another, as your mother and your father do, and your good dear Rebbe! Promise this to him, to your good Rebbe, give him a kiss on the hand and swear to him that if he pardons you, if I pardon you, if your schoolmates pardon you, and if God strengthens your heart, you will never again want to do such a thing."

Yosele kissed the Rebbe's hand, but he couldn't swear.

"Why don't you swear?" Khyene asked.

"Take me home, Mama," Yosele barely managed to say. "My head hurts. Oy, it's getting so dark in this house!"

"Really, take him home, Khyene," the Rebbe advised, seeing how the child's demeanor had changed so suddenly. "I excuse him. There'll be time in the morning for him to promise."

Khyene, weak and dejected, took her wounded child home with her last strength and was soon lying in a bath.

"I hope it had a curative effect," Borekh greeted his wife. "I see, it must have been a good bath, one of blows! This is how I know you are a mother. Otherwise, what then, let him be a thief?"

Khyene wanted to spill out her feelings, but she was so depressed she couldn't let out a single word.

The whole night Yosele burnt like a fire, sleeping restlessly, moaning. A stream of compassion drowned the poor mother's heart. She remembered for the first time that Yosele had not even had a dry crust of bread in his mouth that morning and the whole day, and she herself had beaten and bitten this hungry child, her husband had beaten him so severely, and after that, the Rebbe!

And Yosele's beaten, lashed skin lay before her eyes as in the very moment when the Rebbe gave the first blow. She raised up his little shirt and the world grew dark before her eyes: the skin on his miserable little body was so cut and torn!

"I myself carried my child to the sacrifice!" she cried, lamenting. "I myself brought my child to the altar and prepared the slaughterer's knife! How can you look at this, Master of the Universe, and not console the wounded child and his poor mother with future joy? Why? For what? For nothing! He was foolish once, but he's really just a child. If his mother were Sheyndele and not Khyene, he would never have made this foolish mistake. And even if he had, he wouldn't have been punished so severely. Hold both of us accountable, dear God in Heaven, and send him healing, that he may be healthy and virtuous!"

In the morning, Yosele stood up, although weak as an invalid. When his mother asked, "What hurts?" he answered, "Nothing."

Khyene wanted to keep him home from school, but Borekh shrieked, "He'll go! You're too easy on him! Have you already forgotten what happened yesterday?"

And so Yosele went off to school. But when he arrived, he stopped at the door, afraid to go in. When the other boys saw him, they told the Rebbe. Reb Berl came out, led Yosele inside by the hand, brought him to the table and opened a Khumesh for him.

"Recite!" the Rebbe pointed in the Khumesh and called out the words to him.

"*Thou shalt not steal!*" Yosele read out, and tears fell on the prayer book.

"Again!"

"Thou shalt not steal!" and again, three more times.

"Now take the Khumesh in your hand and swear that you will never steal again."

Yosele swore.

"Remember, you have sworn by the Khumesh," the Rebbe said. "All you boys bear witness. If you ever steal again, I'll strip the flesh off you and afterwards throw you out of school!"

"We bear witness!" the boys called out.

"And nobody will call him thief again, do you hear?" Reb Berl commanded. "Now, come study!"

"And you, fine fellow," the Rebbetzin said to Yosele, "go rock the baby, but don't take anything, do you hear?" To the schoolboys she quietly said: "Children, you must always pay careful attention to him when I leave the house! He's really a good boy, a quiet child, but he has long fingers!"

The gang of boys didn't need to hear any more than this. Little children are so wild at times; no malice is too small to turn to their pleasure. Meeting them in a group, one who has something about his manner or his clothes that unfortunately catches their attention will find them, for no reason at all, suddenly running after him with shouts and uproar, with mud and with stones. Neither kind words nor angry words help at all. They follow the victim as they please, and the fellow should give thanks for an escape without torn clothes or, worse, a hole in the head.

Although Yosele had never provoked a single boy in school, and had always been afraid to respond when he himself was provoked by someone else, and even though the Rebbe had decreed that no one should call him "thief," the boys were not able, by their very nature, to keep from irritating him or holding back anything which would mortify or cause him suffering. Barely had the Rebbe turned away when one or another of them let out the cry: "Thief!"

Mischievous Moyshele even came forward with a string to measure Yosele's fingers and show all the boys that Yosele's fingers were very long. Yosele suffered more from this than from the Rebbe's leather whip, a lot more even than from his rods.

That wasn't all. The schoolboys began to sing Yosele a little song; nobody knew who had thought it up, but all of them sang it: "Yosele's a thief, swats will give him grief, spank him and he'll learn, let's get his hat to burn."

This song cost Yosele more bitter tears. In the same way he'd previously begged God that his mother be as rich as Leybele's mother, his father not cough and curse at him, and his Rebbe not hit him "by accident," now every time he prayed, his little heart cried out: "God, forgive me. I'll never steal again, really never ever. But please let the Rebbetzin stop watching me, and please let my schoolmates not call me thief. Let them not sing that song!"

A few weeks passed, and his mother gradually stopped repeating her words of reproof to him, the words that had taken his last bit of health. Also, his father had almost forgotten the hatred he felt towards him, although in times of great anger, he now added to the words "Peasant" and "Esau," the word "Thief!"

In school the little song was half forgotten, but the Rebbe's leather whip did not forget its "mistakes," and more often than not found Yosele when the Rebbe wanted to take aim at another boy. And although the whip was no better and no softer and hurt Yosele no less than before, nevertheless, one rarely heard a cry or whimper from him.

Yosele took everything for the good: the whip, tending the baby, taking laundry to the river for the Rebbetzin; everything for the good if only he could avoid hearing the name, "Thief," or hearing the little song, the rhyme which hurt more than everything else combined. He was already becoming almost happy, so that he stopped wishing to become rich. Going home, his eyes no longer scanned the ground for treasures, great or small, and he was again studying and wanting to study.

But then, Leybele, beloved only son of Sheyndele the Tax Assessor's wife, brought a pocketknife to school. It was a little pocketknife with an eyeglass through which one could read the whole *Shema Yisroel* prayer. An uncle had sent it to him from abroad as a present.

Looking through the eyeglass, the Rebbe himself was intrigued, and soon showed the Rebbetzin the remarkable sight. She, however, could by no means understand how the whole *Shema Yisroel* could have crept inside such a small pocketknife. The Rebbe labored to explain it as a swindle, a deceit, or the type of telescope in which a greater cleverness lies, but she kept complaining her mind could not take it in.

For an entire day all the boys played with the pocketknife, looking through it with one eye and reading the words, and even Menashe Milner's two sons, who could barely read the prayer book, were able to read through almost half the *Shema Yisroel*. The pocketknife passed from one boy to the next, until the Rebbe finally got angry and ordered Leybele to put the knife away, and Leybele obeyed.

Yosele also wanted to take a look through the eyeglass, and he too asked to see what everyone saw there, but Mischievous Moyshele didn't let him. "Don't show him, Leybele, he'll steal it! You'll see. Remember what I'm telling you!" Moyshele shouted, and Leybele didn't show it to Yosele.

That evening, when the Rebbe and the children had already prayed and said the *Shema Yisroel,* Leybele grabbed at his pocket. "The pocketknife is gone," he cried out. The Rebbe himself helped with the search and looked in all of Leybele's pockets. Nothing!

One boy let out a cry, "Yosele stole the pocketknife!" And Mischievous Moyshele testified that he himself had seen Yosele stick his hand into Leybele's pocket.

"Yosele!" the Rebbe shouted.

"I've sent him to the store for salt!" the Rebbetzin responded. "What is it, why do you need him?"

"I'm afraid a new fiasco is beginning," the Rebbe answered very unhappily. Just at that moment, Yosele came back with a clay cup of salt and gave it to the Rebbetzin along with the change.

"Yosele," the Rebbe said in a falsely friendly manner, "come here, I want to ask you something."

Yosele came, not sensing the black clouds that had suddenly gathered over his poor head.

"Speak up, Yosele," the Rebbe asked, caressing him. "Have you taken Leybele's pocketknife? Perhaps because Leybele called you a thief? That's fine, don't give it to him. Give it to me. I'll never give it back to him. It will stay with me until Leybele swears he'll never hit you, never sing you his silly little song?"

Yosele's little heart sensed something bad was beginning. With tears in his little eyes he answered, "Rebbe, I didn't take the pocketknife. I didn't even see it."

The Rebbe looked him fiercely in the eyes for a few moments. Yosele could not hold the glance and began to cry.

"If you didn't take the pocketknife, why are you crying?" the Rebbe began earnestly. "Your crying is really a sign that you're guilty, so you'd really better give it back, of your own free will, before I get the rods."

"As this is God's holy book, I did not even see the pocketknife!" swore the forlorn child on the Khumesh and all his limbs shivered.

"You didn't see it, but did you *take* it?" asked the Rebbe.

"I also didn't take it!"

"Did you steal it?"

"I also didn't steal it, Rebbe! It's forbidden to steal! I have sworn three times by the Khumesh that I will never steal again. I will never, never steal again."

"One who can steal can also swear falsely. Do you understand, you little bastard?" the Rebbe shouted.

"And if he can steal once, he can steal again!" the Rebbetzin added. "What a pity, such a lovely pocketknife. He'll give it away for a kopeck. Take my advice: shake out his pockets and you'll find it!"

Reb Berl took Yosele's poor little garments and shook them out, then told him to take off his shoes and socks. He took the hat off his head, tapped it inside and out, nothing. And Reb Berl began to believe that perhaps Yosele was not guilty. But Leybele, sobbing over his dear little pocketknife, and Mischievous Moyshele, who more than likely took the knife himself, both cried and swore that Yosele had stolen and buried it somewhere in the courtyard.

"This pocketknife will be an ugly story!" the Rebbe screamed. "It may cost me my life!" And shouting thus he tugged a few sticks out of the broom and laid Yosele on the bench.

"Confess!" shrieked Reb Berl with fury and struck Yosele with rods. "Speak up! Where have you hidden the pocketknife?"

Yosele screamed with pain, but said nothing.

"Confess, rascal," Berl began again, "even your mother won't know. Confess, quickly, where have you hidden the pocketknife?"

Yosele didn't speak but screamed again with his last strength.

"Speak up, quickly, you little thief! Speak or I'll drag you by the ears to your mother. She'll beat you, you'll confess in front of her!" The Rebbe laid the rods again with more force than before.

"Oy Rebbe, I'm dying! Don't beat me any more. I'll tell you already!" screamed the tortured boy.

The Rebbe stopped. "Sha, this opens a path," he said and waited for Yosele to start explaining. But Yosele just cried and said nothing.

"Why don't you speak?" asked Reb Berl, impatiently.

"What should I say?" asked Yosele, sobbing.

"Say where you buried the pocketknife. Speak!"

"I don't know!"

"Again 'I don't know?'" shouted the Rebbe in fury and began to shake him like a *lulav.* "Just wait—you'll soon spill it out. Come with me to your mother, you bastard, to your mother! Let her die, as far as I'm concerned, for having such a dear child.

She should have been struck dumb before I let her override my objections of ever letting you into my school!

Reb Berl shrieked like a wild thing: "Let's go to your mother; I'll let out my anger to her."

And Reb Berl put on his hat, took his walking stick in one hand, grabbed Yosele with the other, and dragged him out of the school.

"Oy, Rebbe, don't take me to Mama! She'll die," Yosele pleaded.

"Then tell me, where have you buried the pocketknife?"

"In the yard, in a little hole!" he answered, just so he wouldn't be taken to his mother.

"Come show me! Where?"

"I'll show you, Rebbe! Don't take me to Mama!"

And the poor child showed the Rebbe where in the yard he had supposedly buried the pocketknife. And he dug in the ground with trembling hands, not even knowing himself what he dug, what he sought.

"Why aren't you finding it?" Reb Berl asked angrily.

"Good Rebbe, dear Rebbe," Yosele suddenly took the Rebbe's hand and began to kiss it, wetting it with bitter tears. "I didn't take the pocketknife. I didn't steal it, I didn't even see it, and I didn't bury it. Under the blue heavens, I swear, and God is my witness, I didn't take the pocketknife! Don't beat me. If you do, God will punish you! He is my witness and He will stand by me!"

Yosele's fiery and moving outburst startled the Rebbe. "Perhaps the child really doesn't know anything," he thought. "Perhaps God himself will really stand up for him!" And he almost began trembling for the punishment which might come to him from all this.

""Well then, who took the knife? There really was a pocket-knife, and Leybele didn't leave the school. Who then is the real thief?"

"I don't know. I don't know, Rebbe!" Yosele replied.

Reb Berl began considering all the children, wondering who was capable of stealing the pocketknife; he remembered that Mischievous Moyshele had the whole time seemed different than usual, not like the other children.

"It could be his work," he said to himself, "but if I start up with him, perhaps I'll find nothing on him, and then my life will be in danger. Itsi Shnitkremer, his father, could put me in jail, or he could come to school and give me a few blows. And even if I do find something on him, I won't be able to do anything about it. So it's bad to find something, but to find nothing is also bitter! If this were an ordinary pocketknife, I'd pay as much as half a ruble from my own pocket to buy Leybele another one! But go choke yourself! And to make things even worse, it had to be a pocketknife with an eyeglass, with a *Shema Yisroel*. Somebody should have broken the hands of that foreigner who made the pocketknife that's bringing me such unhappiness!"

"Come home to your mother," Reb Berl suddenly said to Yosele in a completely different tone. "Tell her no stories about me hitting you. And it really bothers me that perhaps you're not guilty. But I am not guilty either, and Leybele's mother is really going to yell at me."

"Don't take me to Mama, dear Rebbe!" the child begged. "I'm afraid she'll die!"

"If you haven't taken it," consoled Reb Berl, "you don't need to be afraid. She won't hit you, you little fool!"

"Why has the Rebbe whipped and beaten me if I haven't taken it?" the child asked, sobbing.

"Because, after all, I don't know whether you did or not," Reb Berl answered.

"Why has the Rebbe hit only me?" asked Yosele. "Maybe another boy took the pocketknife!"

"You know why I hit only you?" explained the Rebbe. "Because you've already proven yourself to be a thief. Remember? Or perhaps that time it was a lie as well? A boy who has once been caught out stealing shouldn't be angry if people suspect him a second time, even if perhaps falsely. Understand?"

Yosele didn't answer, but his tears began to flow, and saying not another word, he arrived at home, shivering, with the Rebbe.

Khyene sat like stone; she couldn't speak a word as she heard out Berl's narration about the pocketknife. Borekh, however, was soon in a rage, and threw himself at his child and began to beat him.

"Without anger, Reb Borekh," the Rebbe interjected. "Rage makes things worse and you won't get anywhere with him. His mother must explore this with kindness as only a mother can."

"How could a person not be angry? A thief!" the father shouted. "I won't leave him alive. Where's the knife? You hear, you bastard, you thief?" and he attacked Yosele again.

"Away from the child!" Khyene shrieked in a voice not her own. "My bastard, my thief? I'll suffer for him and for you, you wretched father! Just try to lay a finger on him again and whatever falls into my hand will soon be flying towards your head!"

"Very nice, very fine!" said Borekh, coughing. "You see, Reb Berl, who the thief takes after? Speak up, Reb Berl, am I not right?"

"Anger is, in general, an ugly character trait; as soon as you get angry, things get worse," Reb Berl said to him. "Khyene, with your good intent you'll get the whole truth. Just use kindness, I beg you, Khyene, only kindness! Sooner or later, the truth must come out, and perhaps it will be revealed that a different boy, not Yosele, is to blame. Meanwhile, it would be a sin to beat Yosele for no reason."

"I should be so guilty when the time comes for me to stand before the Master of the Universe!" Khyene shouted. "A mother's heart senses when her child is guilty and when he isn't! I don't hold it against you, Rebbe, that you suspect my child. What should a stranger say when his own father says no better? But let his hand wither, he who has stolen the pocketknife and for whose sake my poor child has been tortured! Master of the Universe, show Your truth, Your judgment of the world, and let my curse, this once in my life, fall upon the one who's really earned it!"

"This matter does not belong in cheder," Berl said as if in answer. "Let Yosele come to school tomorrow. The pocketknife will be found. At this point, I myself believe your child doesn't know anything about it. And now, good night!"

Reb Berl left for home, deep in thought. "What will I say to Sheyndele? She'll have plenty to say about her only son's expensive pocketknife stolen at school! And how does one explain to her that the suspect is hardly guilty and perhaps not guilty at all? To tell her Mischievous Moyshele could have taken it? This is all I need!"

Coming back into the school, he didn't find any children. They had all scattered. Leybele, too, who hadn't wanted to wait until the Rebbe came back with the pocketknife, had gone home with eyes swollen from crying. Coming home he had soon told his mother, sobbing, that Yosele, Khyene the sexton's wife's boy, had stolen his pocketknife.

"Yosele is a thief," the precious boy said, "who took money once from the Rebbe himself, the fifty kopecks he was once missing and for the sake of which father beat our servant, Khatskl. The

Rebbetzin says, 'Yosele has long fingers, and if he stretches them out, he can reach into anybody's pocket!'" Those last words Leybele had heard from the cheder boys explaining what "long fingers" meant.

"Why haven't you ever told me this?" the mother asked. "That Yosele, an evil death may he die, is a thief?" "If I had known, he wouldn't have stayed in the school this long, and your pocket-knife wouldn't have been stolen."

"The Rebbe didn't want us to denounce him," Leybele cried as he told her. "All the boys swore not to tell the story outside of school. Today when the Rebbe beat him, he promised to give it up at his home."

Sheyndele became furious as she heard out her precious child's bitter news. She wanted to run to reckon with Berl, but her husband stopped her. "Take some time," he said. "It's possible the Rebbe will soon bring back the knife."

"Do you think I'm too lazy to go over to Khyene the thief's mother's house?" Sheyndele shrieked. "If the Rebbe doesn't bring it back, she herself will have to give it back to me, even if she's sick. What a sorry comedown! She swore with such oaths and curses that her bastard wouldn't touch even a kopeck of my child's money or a bite of his lunch. And I was such a fool to let her talk me around. I put in a word with the Rebbe for her bastard, to let him into the school. And now he deceives and steals everything my child brings with him, and then takes it home to his mother! Try to figure anybody out these days! She speaks, it appears, with God, and then teaches her child to steal from cheder boys and brings the loot into her house!"

"I've long told you," Reb Shloyme responded, "a pauper is a thief! If a pauper comes to you, let him stand by the door; give him his alms if you have a good heart, then let him leave in good health! If Khyene or another such woman, well-spoken and well-educated, comes to you, shove a couple of groschen into her hand and then out she goes! You, however, are no better than all the other women. Someone like Khyene comes in, an inferior; you take her in, give her the seat of honor. You have dealings with her. You hear out her invented stories: that she has a son with a fine head, that she wants him to study Torah. You believe her and tell our only son's Rebbe to take the boy into school, into our Leybele's cheder! Some friend! 'There's nothing like them,' say the wives, and they're right."

"All right, all right, I'll get even with her!" responded Sheyndele, angered by his moralizing. "She'll be a sick woman by the time she's given up the pocketknife to me, and her foot will never again cross my threshold. What have I got to fear from her? That she may swear and sob? That she has quite a mouth on her? May her oaths fall into the ocean and be sent back to her! Vain oaths, worthless, may they never find their target!"

"But why should you put up with this?" said her husband, not ceasing to lecture her. "Are you simply trying to be a good person? One should not be good to paupers! Even if you give them the shirt off your back, you still can't solve their troubles. It's really simpler not to have any contact with them from the very beginning. Khyene was treated well, you gave her so much, this is the thanks she gives you. Now she'll gossip and curse you. Serves you right!"

"She won't have any more of what's yours!" Sheyndele threw back at her husband. "I know you think I give to Khyene from your grandmother's inheritance, but she's had no more from me than a coin in exchange for last year's Yom Kippur candles. I want you to know, if I'd known how far she would fall, I'd have chased her from my house with sticks." And thus they did a good bit of arguing through the night, man and wife, until Leybele, crying, fell asleep.

# Eight

Reb Berl, coming back from Khyene's, had also warred with his wife for a good hour. She kept shouting that he was a rag, a clay wagon shaft, that he now believed Yosele didn't take the pocketknife because Khyene, with her polished little tongue, may it be cut off, has explained it all away. "If not Yosele, you big fool with a long beard," she shrieked, "if Yosele didn't take it, it'll turn out that you or I was the thief!"

Berl was afraid to say that any boy at school could have taken the knife as easily as Yosele. That even a *tzaddik,* were he made a boy, would find it hard to resist the temptation of such an ingenious knife. And that it was clear to him that more than anybody, Mischievous Moyshele almost certainly took it.

"A woman has a long tongue and she will gossip about this," he thought to himself, and did not disclose his suspicions about Mischievous Moyshele.

"He would have confessed to a different teacher!" the Rebbetzin persisted.

"No condemned prisoner could have been beaten more than I beat Yosele!" Berl answered. "You yourself, I recall, were standing there, and you saw! And just imagine, you foolish woman, when it turns out the poor child happens not to be guilty, do you think God will remain silent before such an undeserved wounding of a guiltless soul?"

"But what will you say to Sheyndele? Don't you know you're playing with fire?" she complained to her husband.

"That's absolutely what's on my mind," Berl groaned, and he couldn't sleep all night from grief.

Khyene slept peacefully and well all night, almost better than ever before. After Reb Berl's departure she had carefully interrogated Yosele, both kindly and in anger, in case he knew even a little bit about the pocketknife. When she had deduced from his answers that he was completely guiltless, from beginning to end, she cried herself out, seeing how cut and torn his skin was. She kissed him well, thanked God that her child was not a thief, laid herself down to sleep and didn't move till dawn.

In the morning, she sent Yosele to school and told him he shouldn't lose courage. God would see his unearned pain and troubles, and the truth would come out.

The Rebbe didn't say a word to him, neither in kindness nor in anger, but Leah the Rebbetzin took to diplomatic interrogation, hoping she could accomplish with words what her husband had not accomplished with rods and blows.

"Speak up, you thief, you'll suffer for this. You really won't give back the pocketknife? May God give you agony enough for all Jews!"

Yosele only looked at her, but did not answer.

"Why are you mute? You'll really be a mute, I tell you!"

"I didn't steal the pocketknife. I didn't even see it," Yosele answered briefly and to the point.

"May you see no more light before your eyes, as you really did see the knife! Wait, wait, you bastard, little thief, I'll get you! Your Rebbe isn't worthy to walk around in this world if he keeps such a thief in school!"

Yosele just looked at the foolish woman, whom he had always obeyed through fire and water, and in that moment hated her more for her words than he hated the Rebbe for all his beatings.

Suddenly the door burst open and Sheyndele and her only son Leybele came in. Sheyndele, a fat Jewess with a three-story double chin and a string of big pearls around her neck, was as red as fire. She was so angry she even forgot to say, "Good morning," when the Rebbe greeted her.

"I've certainly done well, Rebbe! This is what comes from the kindness I did you. Letting you enroll a thief in my son's school. A poor child, a *shlepper,* let's not say it out loud. Where is the Rebbe? I mean: where are you, Reb Berl? Where is your guidance, your supervision, what are you getting paid for? Fine supervision! A Rebbe thinks it right to take in a bastard, a thief, seemingly so the children can learn all his evil tricks."

"Sit down, Sheyndele, calm your self a little," the Rebbe said, bringing her a bench and wiping the dust off it with the edge of his robe.

"I didn't come here to sit with you," Sheyndele began to expound further. "I came to get the pocketknife even if it costs me half a life. This isn't about the pocketknife itself, even though it's an expensive, foreign pocketknife, about which you are no expert. How do you come to be an expert about such a thing? Have you ever been abroad in your entire life? I would sacrifice this pocketknife for my Leybele's least fingernail. There's nothing I would take in exchange for his crying and sobbing the entire night. Let the life of Khyene's bastard be taken away as he has taken away a bit of my only son's health! What do I need this for? What good came to me, that you should have such a one in your school? It's you who are guilty, Rebbe! I'm a woman; what did I know? I thought: since you allowed him in your school, you probably knew he was an honest child. Now see how honest! But what am I saying, 'Now'? For three weeks already, you've known he was a thief. What a paragon! He took money from you yourself. All the children knew it and called him thief, but you made them swear not to speak out, and that's what I'll never forgive you for! A fine story, I declare. 'Not speak out.' One tells a child to say nothing when a Rebbe gives him an occasional blow, a lashing. But to not speak out when there is a thieving boy in school, a bum? No, Rebbe, I don't understand this at all."

"Sheyndele, calm yourself," Reb Berl entreated. "You're completely right! But I wasn't guilty either. A child, I thought, does a foolish thing once, and I beat him very thoroughly for it in front of his mother's eyes. And I didn't take him for a thief. A quiet child, ask all the children, has he ever even touched a hair on any head? Now this pocketknife, this is really an ugly story, but I still don't know if he stole it, even if in general it was stolen at all. Perhaps Leybele lost it somewhere?"

"All angry nightmares on my enemies' heads!" Sheyndele spit and threw herself at the Rebbe. "What do you mean by this, Rebbe? Do you think I'm a babe in the woods that you want to ridicule me like this? You think I don't know that he's confessed, that he gave it to his mother? I hope all sicknesses and distress that were intended for me, my husband, and my only son will go to her! I thought you had already retrieved the knife, and Leybele believed this, too, that the Rebbe, when he got back to the school, would give back the knife. And I only came here to speak out my grievance that you had let a thief into your school, and really to see that before my eyes you would drive him away. But now I hear the Rebbe himself ridicules me completely. Where did I get the idea, you say, that the thief had stolen? When a robbery takes place, it seems from your words, one should first suspect the rabbi and only afterwards the bathhouse attendant? Or perhaps, first, my Leybele is the thief, or the other respectable children, and only later will you think, perhaps Khyene's bastard and thief took the pocketknife! Feh, shame on you, Rebbe! He confessed, so why do you want to convince me you still don't know he stole it?"

"When I beat him, he apparently confessed," the Rebbe explained, "but he himself sincerely didn't know what he was confessing to."

"What a beating that probably was!" Sheyndele said with bitter laughter. "What transpired from the speech? I see really that you stand up for him, steel and iron. Do you think he'll stay in your school after this? I tell you, don't think that will happen. Unless you want my Leybele to leave your school after today? And with God's help, what Sheyndele does so will Esterl, Sorele, and Khavele—and not one decent mother will let her child go to your school! You want to keep him? Good health to you! If yours is a school of good-for-nothing thieves, lowlifes, and bastards, perhaps you'll make a better wage than as a teacher of respectable, upstanding children. But that has nothing to do with the pocketknife. The whole world may have to be turned upside down, but I'll have the pocketknife! Where is that thief? Show him to me. I'll show you a trick; he'll give it to me."

"Yosele!" the Rebbe shouted, "come here!"

Yosele came, the little teeth chattering in his head from terror.

"This is him?" Sheyndele looked him over and spit. "You think I can't get it out of this little *shlepper*? Leybele cried all night over this thief? We'll see if I get it out of him or not! A soldier once confessed to stealing from me; I hit him again and again, and he carried my things back into the house. Will this little bastard not also confess?"

Sheyndele suddenly shrieked at Yosele, "Give that knife here, you thief!" And with her full hand, she laid a slap over his whole little face. "Give up that knife! If you don't, your foul little bones will scatter under my hands!" And not seeing that blood had begun to pour from his little nose, she beat him further, tearing and shrieking, "Give the pocketknife here, I won't let up on you until I have the pocketknife!"

Reb Berl, afraid she would kill the child right there in his school, entreated her, "Sheyndele, I beg you, let up on him. How much is the pocketknife worth? Half a ruble? Take it out of your school fee. I'll expel him from school as you demand; just don't hit another's child. He's already been beaten enough. He's been tortured."

"So drive him out, already! There should be no trace of him here, starting now!" And not waiting for the Rebbe to do it, she gave the bloodied child another blow and threw him out the door. "Get out!" she shrieked. "Never cross this threshold again, you thief!"

"Leah," the Rebbe called to his wife, "go take him into the yard and wash the blood off him."

"What are you afraid of?" Sheyndele shrieked. "I don't intend to damage my hands. I would hit the face of his mother herself because she received stolen goods through her child's thievery! This was her whole intent, really, the reason she sent him to your school! Oh, yes, he would learn Torah. Some fine fellow he turns out to be in the world! He was going to be a thief, and she found no better place for him to do it than in your school! Come home, Leybele, you won't study today. I'll buy you a better pocketknife. With that other pocketknife let them stab themselves, Master of the Universe, for my child's grief and tears, poor thing!"

# NINE

Yosele came home bloodied and swollen. His mother barely recognized him.

"Was it the Rebbe again?" she asked fearfully, "who hit you this way? He'll be beaten by God."

"It wasn't the Rebbe, Mama!" the child answered. "Leybele's mother beat me. She thrashed me to make me give back the pocketknife—the pocketknife I never even saw."

"And your good Rebbe let her beat you right there in his school?"

"He didn't want to let her. It was *she* who beat me and drove me out of the school!" he said, crying ever harder. "Oy, Mama, why does God let me be beaten so unjustly? He surely knows I'm no thief at all, that I didn't even see the pocketknife!"

Khyene trembled with rage. Her face became pale. She bit her lips with her teeth, and not answering her bloodied child's question, she grabbed him by the hand and said, "Come, my poor child! Come as you are, beaten and bloodied, to Sheyndele. Let the whole world see how one beats someone else's poor child for no reason at all! Come, I'll lay what's in my pained, bitter heart on her head! May she know that a poor child also has a mother and isn't a deserted stray that people can beat and bloody as they please to their cruel hearts' desire. *She* drives my child out of the cheder? God will drive her soul right out of her fat body!"

"And I tell you, Khyene, don't go!" Borekh interjected. "Don't go, don't mix it up with the rich folks! They have no God in their hearts. And how can a poor man stand against a rich one?" But Khyene wouldn't listen.

Sheyndele and her husband were sitting at the table eating breakfast when Khyene came into their house. Sheyndele believed that Khyene had come to bring back the pocketknife, and she cried out happily, "Who's right? I said, 'The knife will be brought back to our house.' I always said Khyene is a respectable woman and won't want her child to be a thief!"

"My child is no thief, Sheyndele," Khyene called out. "And certainly no bastard either!"

Her heart was so crushed she could barely speak another word although she had plenty to say.

"Who said, God forbid, a bastard?" Sheyndele asked.

"*You*, Sheyndele! You beat my poor child worse than a bastard! People should see how a woman has the heart to beat and bloody someone else's poor child. Why? What did he do to you? What did he do to your child? How can one have so little of God in her heart as to believe a mother can see this happen and ignore it? You, Sheyndele, are a rich woman and don't know the pain and suffering a poor mother carries in her heart!"

"So let him not be a thief and then I wouldn't have had to beat him. I shouldn't have let him out of my hands alive. Let him just give back the pocketknife. Let sickness and troubles be given to him!"

"Nobody is guaranteed exemption from troubles, Sheyndele! Don't think just because you're the rich one and I the poor that I'm afraid of you. I don't have such a bad heart in me that I would beat your child or even curse him as you've beaten and cursed my child. But I pray to God that He pay you back, pay *you,* not your child, that your hand wither and dry up, that *you* shall be beaten by God and no doctor or healer be able to help you. Your blood shall flow from your heart and your neck as my poor child's blood has flowed under your hand!"

"Quiet, hussy!" Reb Shloyme the Taxman shouted. "Khatskl," he called to the servant, "take this trollop by the hair and throw her out the door like a dog!"

"Khatskl," Sheyndele called out as well, "it was for the sake of this little thief that you took two blows from the man of the house! It was this boy who stole the half-ruble from the Rebbe, and people suspected you and gave you undeserved blows. Now you can get even for those indignities! Why should I be bothered by the curses she's laid on me? Why listen when a worm-tongue barks? What impertinence from such a low-life!"

"Khatskl, a ruble a smack!" Reb Shloyme offered. "I'll give you two rubles in cash for the two smacks I gave to you rather than to that little bastard back then. Just teach this pauper a lesson for her presumption, that she came into my house to curse my wife who was just being a good Jew by keeping her and her thieving son out of the Gentiles' hands."

"Liar, show yourself!" Khatskl shouted. "See, boss, 'the end of a thief is the gallows.' Here I'll avenge myself for my disgraces and undeserved blows!"

With this speech he started to throw himself on Yosele and his mother, but Khyene grabbed a candlestick, which stood near her hand, and threw it at him. Khatskl ducked his head and the candlestick flew into a mirror, which crashed to the floor in pieces. Khatskl got wild, and before Khyene had time to grab something to defend herself from him, he had seized her and beat her with his fists on her back, her chest, anywhere he could find. Khyene bit him and this drove Khatskl even wilder.

Reb Shloyme opened a window, stuck out his head, and shouted, "Police! A fight!"

Sheyndele had a seizure. She cried and hiccupped. Leybele shouted with fear. People came running in from the street.

Khatskl was torn away from Khyene, and his first act was to lay a blow on the despairing Yosele. "There, you'll also taste the flavor of the honor I've bestowed on your mother!" he said.

A policeman came in and found the house full of people, men and women, big and small. Bloodied, beaten people, a broken mirror, overturned chairs, everybody talking, everybody shrieking, and it was hard to understand a single word.

Soon a police captain came, people took off their hats, and after a while it became quiet. Reb Shloyme told the whole history: Here is the little bastard, Yosele, who has always been known as a thief and has now stolen a pocketknife. And here is his mother, who is no better than he is, and who taught him to steal. "She came to me in my house, made such a scandal, broke an expensive mirror, terrified the whole family, bit and bloodied Khatskl. And why, I myself don't even know!"

The police captain asked for pen and ink, wrote out a report, and asked Khyene: "Who are you? What's your name? What's your employment?" He also asked Yosele to state how long he had been employed in the occupation of thievery. Khyene didn't answer any of his questions. Yosele simply did not understand the question.

The police captain read over the report. Reb Shloyme signed it and the police captain took mother and child away to the police station.

Sheyndele kept having spasms until a doctor came and sent for a pharmacist. Sheyndele calmed down and put herself to bed sick with a bandaged head. Afterwards, the doctor also bound up Khatskl's bloody hand and advised him to avoid dangerous work until his wound was completely healed.

People dispersed to share the unusual events they had seen with their own eyes and heard with their own ears; the gossip cooked and clanged around town. People were already willing to believe Khyene's Yosele was a thief, but that Khyene should be so impertinent as to come to Shloyme and his wife in their home and curse them, and further, to confront such rich folk head-on, to break an expensive mirror worth a hundred rubles, and to mix it up with Khatskl the Servant, a man with strength enough to throw a big healthy butcher out of the house, was to everyone a wonder of wonders. If one weren't able to say they'd seen it with their own eyes, perhaps nobody would've believed it. But as proof that it was true, Khyene had been taken to jail and locked up.

It even seemed possible that Khyene had been in the right. Not because they knew why she did it, but simply because people hated Reb Shloyme and loathed Sheyndele even more. There was a lot of talk about it in the study house after evening prayers.

"Listen, people," Yoyne the Water Carrier said, "this is how it is: Khyene and her son are locked up in jail. But as for Reb Borekh and his twins, it's a desolation. I took him a pail of water today and saw how he tries to take care of them, poor things. He swore to me he hadn't had anything in his mouth, not him, not his twins. He didn't even know his wife was in prison. I told him and he coughed so much I thought he was done for. When he came to himself, he cried, 'I told her she shouldn't go fight with a rich woman!' He was right, but it's still a great pity."

"People," called out Reb Shoyel the Slaughterer, a very respected man in the study house. "One shouldn't hear out only one side of a story! You all know, after all, that I enter the Taxman's house almost every day, and I can tell you, the story went like this: Khyene's little boy studied with Reb Berl. Sheyndele's little boy also studies with Reb Berl. Reb Shloyme's son brought a pocketknife to school. Khyene's boy, people say, stole the pocketknife. Sheyndele bloodied Khyene's boy. Khyene cursed Sheyndele for it. Shloyme stood up for his wife and told Khatskl to beat Khyene. Khatskl beat her. Khyene broke a mirror, and the upshot is, Khyene is now in jail!

"So this is the heart of the matter: Borekh and his twins, who everyone will agree are not guilty, are simply dying of hunger. And since it's a good deed, 'the ransoming of prisoners,' and since the prisoner is the wife of a sick man, a mother of infants, it's a crime to let them die from hunger; therefore, it is only right that some Jews should go to the higher-ups, even if it costs a bit of money, and get Khyene freed, and it will be a mitzvah if we all help out. I'll give a gulden."

"To spite Sheyndele, may she have a downfall," a butcher spoke up, "I give two. If people give even one gulden, it will make, all told, a few rubles."

People gave as much as they could. A couple of volunteers were found who would undertake to speak with the police chief, and they went off to the police station.

They discovered Khyene and her son had been released just an hour earlier. It wasn't known why, but it was declared that the police chief, even though an aristocrat and strict man, didn't have the heart, after seeing her spitting blood and deathly sick from Khatskl's blows, to imprison the impoverished, unlucky woman or her badly beaten child.

The rubles collected from the assembly following evening prayers were put to good use. Khyene was sick for a full week and couldn't go out in the street to earn a living. The few rubles earned by her eldest daughter, a twelve-year-old girl whom she had apprenticed with a ladies' tailor the previous year, were keeping the whole little family alive.

Neighbors were coming around to ask after Khyene's health, sometimes bringing something for the hungry children, but every time reproving Yosele, pointing out it was his fault his mother had sickened and that the situation would not have become so dire if he, Yosele, weren't a thief.

"My child is not a thief!" Khyene repeated over and over. "I beg you, don't give him a bad name. If he were actually a thief, I would never have come to this state!" Every time she said these words, her tears flowed.

There were those who advised Khyene to lodge a complaint against Sheyndele and Reb Shloyme, to call a doctor and show him how sick she was, spitting blood because they had beaten her so badly in their home. For such a thing, they said, people can be sent to Siberia. But Khyene answered, "God will judge them. I'll never prevail here among men."

When Khyene was able to get out of bed and was out in the street for the first time, the first thing she did was to seek a new Rebbe for Yosele. But she sought in vain. In vain she asked each teacher to ask Reb Berl: hadn't she repaid him to the very last kopeck? Would he say Yosele was really a thief, a name only Sheyndele had made for him in the town?

Her begging did not help. Regarding tuition, Reb Berl openly said Khyene had paid him with more honor than did the rich; but as to the matter of Yosele being a thief, he answered, "It's better to stay silent. A pity." And although Berl had perhaps meant with his words completely the opposite, nevertheless, no teacher wanted to take even a possible thief into his class, especially since all the schoolboys knew about Yosele; and when they met him would shout, "Yosele the thief! Here's the pocketknife thief!"

This sapped Khyene's last bit of strength, but she couldn't let the boy come back and study with his father as before. Borekh, who had previously been merely an angry, harsh father to him, was now a real danger to his life. "Because of him," Borekh grumbled all day long, "that peasant, that thief, we'll all be laid in the earth before our time!"

Khyene had to take Yosele with her wherever she went so as not to leave him alone with his father, who bore him such unwarranted hatred. She no longer had the will, as she once had, to fight or argue with her husband. It was hard for her to talk, and the doctor said any argument or anxiety was a danger to her.

But where could she avoid anxiety? Even in the street, thanks to her child, little schoolboys ran after her and cried, "There goes Yosele the thief, Yosele the pocketknife thief!" They sometimes pelted her and her child with mud and stones. And once, a very fine housewife from whom Khyene had often earned a few gulden, said it was offensive that she brought Yosele along with her when she came.

"You're really not guilty, Khyene my dear," she consoled her, "but what mother can guarantee her child? Nothing can be done about such a nature. It's too late! An adult can sometimes hold himself back, my husband says, but a small child can't. If it strikes him to take something he'll take it. A thousand mothers wouldn't make a difference."

Khyene was so mortified by this speech she was literally unable to speak a single word. She just raised her tear-filled eyes to the heavens, and her heart cried out, "My poor despondent child! Answer, God—You know the real truth!"

One morning, a bailiff brought a summons, "She is called with her Yosele to the court of justice," he said, and demanded that Khyene sign the papers.

Khyene brought the papers to a neighbor, who signed for her and explained that she was accused of making a scandal at the home of Shloyme Ayzenharts, breaking a mirror and assaulting the servant. It further accused her, with her son, of various acts of robbery.

Khyene became pale and frightened, but she soon found her courage and said: "So it goes! What can the judge do to me? Nobody can die twice, but everyone must die once! My death, as I see it, won't be long in coming. Already I have no heart, no lungs. Every moment I feel I'll go out like a light. And what do I care about that? It's probably my destiny. Let my Angel of Death be Sheyndele. She'll have the mitzvah of taking a woman before her time, a wife from a sick man, a mother from tiny infants, poor things! I hold no grudge against her for the deed. May her mitzvah stand her in good stead, Master of the Universe, on the Judgment Day!"

Some people strongly advised Khyene to go to Shloyme and Sheyndele, to fall with tears in her eyes and entreat them to have pity and forgive her so it would not come to a formal trial. But Khyene answered, "It's before the Living God that I fall every minute with a broken heart, beaten down, hoping He'll forgive my sin and lengthen my years so I can continue to be a mother to my children, and at least get them standing on their own little feet. My heart cries to Him! Let Him protect my Yosele from all evils, and further, from evil people who have given him such a cruel name. And if He doesn't answer me, what answer can fat, sinful Sheyndele give me? Things can't get any worse for me. At least let me know, before my death, that I haven't bowed down to false gods."

There were even some who took the mitzvah upon themselves to beg Reb Shloyme on poor sick Khyene's behalf, to pardon her, or to have the Rabbi render a verdict and not make her go to court, saying to him that she was, after all, a woman of good family, the daughter of Reb Yosele the Preacher, a good, pious, respectable woman. They told Shloyme that, from that day forward, she had been spitting blood from the place where Khatskl had struck her lungs, and that she had paid many times over for her impudence; but Reb Shloyme answered, "Everybody is ready for somebody else to be the good one, the one who lets things slide, who is mild! But if you were in my place, if Khyene had done this to you and not to me, wouldn't you have done a thousand times worse against her than I have? What nerve she had to come into my house to curse my wife with death oaths right in front of my eyes! Why? Because her boy is a thief and a bastard!

"And as if that weren't enough, she grabs a candlestick and breaks my expensive mirror causing a loss of over a hundred rubles. And then you want me to say to her, 'Thanks, Khyene, you've done well?' No, one has to teach these paupers the proper respect owed to an upstanding householder. One must teach these dogs some manners! If we make a gift to Khyene today, tomorrow Zeligl the Shoemaker will come, Pinye the Tailor, and Itzikl the Blacksmith will be all over me. Let these paupers, these dogs, see I'll take no pity, even on a woman, and that it doesn't even matter to me that she comes from a respected lineage. Let them see you can't be a scoundrel against a wealthy man!"

Khyene prepared herself for court. She did not draft a counterargument, she did not hire a lawyer; she only called her eldest daughter home from the tailor so there would at least be somebody to cook dinner once in a while for her husband and poor children, if there should be any food to cook at all. For herself, going to court, she took nothing more than her prayer books.

"Goodbye, everyone," she said, crying to her family. "I'm going to jail; the road is broad going in but narrow coming out! Only God knows if I'll survive to come back to my home again.

I give myself over to His hands. Let Him also be your mother, as He is the father of all orphans! You are all, even your sick father, living orphans. God will have pity on you. If I've sinned against Him, let Him strike me alone. I won't say His judgment is wrong, God forbid. Only let Him not abandon you, desolate orphans. Let Him not take His loving kindness and compassion away from you. Be healthy, all of you!"

And after that, she cried over her infants' cradle, kissed them thoroughly, asked the eldest girl to watch over her father and take care of the children. Then she took Yosele by the hand, kissed the mezuzah, and was away to court.

For three hours Khyene sat and waited, then she was called before the judge. Neither Shloyme, nor his wife, were there; she only noticed Reb Berl the teacher, his wife, and a few other people. She wondered why Sheyndele wasn't there. Finally the judge began to read the police report and Shloyme the Tax Assessor's complaint. Khyene listened closely.

"Do you plead guilty to these accusations?" the judge asked when he had finished reading.

"I confess," she answered, "that I cursed Sheyndele in her house because she beat my poor child and bloodied him. I am a mother! Your Honor, if you were to show me a mother who would let her child be beaten and bloodied and not do as I did, I'd spit in her face and say, 'You're no mother!'"

"And did you break the mirror?" the judge asked.

"It wasn't the mirror I wanted to break. It really hurt my heart when it happened, such a pity!" she answered, "What I wanted to break was Khatskl the servant's head because he threw himself on me and my child like an angry dog after his fine master told him to."

"Then do you not know it's forbidden to punch someone's head?" the judge asked.

"Why wouldn't I know that? I know perfectly well," she began to speak with fire. "I know one shouldn't even begin to lay a hand on another. Is there anyone in the world who can say I've ever before raised a hand to anyone since I was born?" She turned to the public. "Speak, Jews! Why are you silent? Are you all really so afraid of Sheyndele?"

The judge brought it to her attention that she must speak only to him and that the public had no right to answer a question unless he himself asked it.

"Very well," said Khyene, "but will the honorable judge tell us what he himself would do if he were set upon by an evil dog that could tear him to pieces?"

"But it wasn't a dog that fell upon you, it was a person!" the judge answered.

"A person! He's some fine person!" Khyene interrupted bitterly. "There are plenty of people, may God not punish me for my words, who are angrier and worse than dogs! And as I pray to God every morning that He shall raise me up away from evil acquaintances, I don't beg him to save me from angry dogs, but from an evil neighbor and bad people. It would be better to meet up with ten dogs than one Khatskl at Sheyndele's house. And you say Khatskl is a man? Is it forbidden to throw a candlestick at his head when he falls on an unhappy, poor, weak woman who has never spoken one word to him?"

The judge was silent but wrote for a few minutes.

"Besides the mirror you broke and the scandal you created," the judge spoke further, "your twelve-year-old son is accused of several thefts. Once he was caught red-handed stealing from his Rebbe, Berl Shatz, and, a few more times, stealing various household items from the Rebbetzin. And after that, he was accused by Shloyme Ayzenharts' seven-year-old son of stealing an expensive pocketknife, and by others, various things. And you are accused of being aware of these robberies and of taking and keeping the items stolen by your boy. Do you confess?"

"Your Honor," Khyene answered with fire, "what I've done, I have not denied, and I've told why I did it. I don't know anything about thievery, and my child doesn't either. It's a lie! Evidence that it's a lie is that my enemies have testified that my Yosele is twelve years old. Well, Your Honor, here's my child. Is he more than seven? The truth is, that not really knowing what he was doing, he once brought his poor hungry mother fifty kopecks from school and said he'd found them. My husband quickly realized he hadn't 'found' them, and it's only because I managed to tear my son from his father's hands that he was spared to be here today!

"I myself also beat my dear child. I bit him, tore at him, and became wild and crazy in an instant from the thought of my child being a thief. I dragged him back to school, put the money right back in the Rebbe's hands, and held my child's little feet while the Rebbe smite him for his foolishness—worse than one smites an adult criminal—until I fainted.

"Can the Rebbe himself say even one of my words is false? Where is he? I saw him here before." She turned again to the audience. "Reb Berl, why don't you tell the truth?"

"He'll testify soon," the judge calmed her. "I'll question him later. And concerning the other robberies?"

"I know absolutely nothing about any other robberies, Your Honor. I swear by the poverty and pain in my heart."

The judge had one of the witnesses called up, the storekeeper to whom the Rebbetzin always used to send Yosele, and she testified that people were always shoplifting in her store. Sometimes candy, sometimes expensive merchandise, sometimes, very often, money was missing from the drawer. But she'd never said it was Yosele who'd done it, because he used to present himself as a poor little fellow who couldn't even count to two. But since she'd found out he'd been able to take money from his own Rebbe, she'd done the right thing and protected herself from him as she would from fire!

"But can one protect oneself from a thief?" the storekeeper asked innocently. "There's more stealing, and I'll be missing more and better things, and it's all his work!"

"Did you ever catch him with something stolen?" asked the judge.

"If I'd caught him with something in his hand, I'd think he'd never have stolen again!" the storekeeper answered. "That's why I'm so angry at him. Because I could never catch him!"

"You may sit down," the judge told the shopkeeper, and he had the other witnesses summoned.

The other witnesses said the whole town knew for a long time that Yosele was a thief and would rip things right out of your hands, and that when he walked in the street boys ran after him and shouted, "Yosele the thief!" A couple of them said, further, that they had suffered a few thefts themselves, had grabbed the thief to beat him, and it seemed to them it was Yosele, but they didn't exactly remember.

The judge asked them, "When? What? How?" But from the stuttering and stammering in their replies, one could see these were simply the kind of witnesses you could buy "three for a ruble," and he told them to sit down.

Finally Reb Berl was called. Khyene's eyes burned; it was obvious all her hopes were pinned on his testimony.

But Reb Berl turned away from her so she couldn't look him in the eye. He stated that, though he had never caught Yosele red-handed with the fifty kopecks, he nevertheless couldn't say he wasn't a thief, because the boy himself admitted he'd stolen the pocketknife and hidden it somewhere; and that after he'd driven Yosele from the school, his wife looked around and saw that many household items were missing, but that he would plead clemency for the boy because he knows the child was almost always hungry all day as he sat in school, and hunger can bring a person to anything.

"Reb Berl," Khyene gave a cry with a voice not her own, and people saw all her limbs give a shudder. "You are afraid to tell the truth in front of Sheyndele, afraid she'll take away your position as teacher. Why aren't you afraid of God to tell such a lie? To lie before God, Reb Berl, who knows the truth and can unmake you? Remember that you are now ruining a poor, guiltless child! The Day of Judgment will come soon, and you will stand before Him, who sees into your heart now. Tell the truth!"

Reb Berl was silent.

"You're silent? Good, you've buried my child and me," Khyene began again. "You'll leave here and go home to your wife and children while I and my innocent child will go like thieves straight to prison. But God hears. May this whole assembly hear that I go to prison with a much cleaner heart than you take to your home!"

Berl's wife's testimony was even worse. She ranted on about what a dear woman Sheyndele was, that she had a good heart and couldn't even see when a child had a suspicious demeanor, and that Sheyndele literally gave Yosele no more than a gentle pat, and that if blood started to flow from his little nose, she herself doesn't know who is guilty. "It astonished me," the Rebbetzin continued, "how even-tempered Sheyndele was; that although Yosele stole the pocketknife, which she herself heard him admit, and although he's a thief who tears things straight out of your hand, nevertheless, Sheyndele gave him no more than a touch, and asked no more than that he not be allowed back in school."

The judge reminded her a couple of times that she should speak to the point and not tell stories unrelated to the current charges, but the Rebbetzin continued as she pleased and went on to describe how she knew that Yosele was a thief. Khyene listened quietly to all this and answered not a word.

"Have you, perhaps, anything to say to this?" the judge asked Khyene.

"I wish to say, Your Honor, that here in court is the first time I've realized how low and false people can be. It's here that I've first realized a poor woman is weaker than a fly when accused by a rich woman like Sheyndele! So I ask you, Your Honor, to judge me quickly. I have nothing more to say."

"Would you perhaps like to agree on some sort of compensation to make peace for the scandal and the broken mirror?" the judge asked.

"I don't understand how," Khyene asked in turn.

"You could, for instance, beg pardon of Shloyme and his wife, or come to some sort of understanding," the judge patiently clarified.

"I should beg pardon of Sheyndele? Beg pardon because she beat and bloodied my poor child and ruined his reputation across the entire town, so no teacher wants to take him into school? Beg pardon of Reb Shloyme, who set his wild servant upon me, forcing me to break the mirror, afterwards punching my lung? No, Your Honor! I don't worry much what will happen to me. But the misery of my small desolate children when I die before my time, thanks to all this, that is my whole concern and the matter I will place before God, the True Judge, when my hour comes. How shall I be false before Him, who sees my heart, and beg pardon, supposedly, of my murderers, the murderers of my whole unhappy family? I ask you, Your Honor, judge me! Punish me, if you decide I am guilty!" And pointing towards Heaven with her hand, she said further, "But up there, with the living God, there is also a judgment! And of His judgment I have more hope now than ever!"

"And what do you say?" the judge asked Sheyndele's lawyer.

"I am empowered only to ask for a verdict. Such a low woman who has the impudence to make a scandal with the most important people in town, to revile and curse such a worthy woman as Sheyndele in her own home, such a one deserves in this case no pity, and I ask that she be punished as strictly as possible."

Khyene, who had been agitated and had waited the whole time for Sheyndele to argue against her, had not imagined that the man standing to the right of the lectern, butting in, interrogating the witnesses and correcting them by adding what they didn't say, was a lawyer for Sheyndele's side. She thought he was some kind of judge, too, but now, when she saw how he stood upholding Sheyndele's honor, she shrieked, "Your Honor, who is this? This is the first time I've seen him in my life. What does he want from me?"

The judge patiently explained the lawyer's role to her.

"Oh, it's like that?" Khyene spoke over him. "I see that until now I've lived in error. I've heard talk about lawyers who plead for those who are accused and who defend them in court, but now I see a lawyer can also be here and there. All you need to do is pay him to make treyf kosher, and he'll make treyf kosher. If another pays him to make kosher treyf, he'll do that, too. That's how it seems!" The public began to laugh, but the judge got angry.

Khyene began again with bitter laughter: "It's certainly easier to bury someone with another's hands than to smear the burial place of a poor woman and her little family yourself! The rich man can afford anything. So when Reb Shloyme wanted me beaten, he told his servant Khatskl to throw me down the stairs. And now that he wants to destroy me completely, he has his lawyer do it. Why would he need to dirty his kosher hands with my blood when he can get a butcher to slaughter treyf as easily as kosher?

"I understand this perfectly well, Mr. Lawyer, but what I don't understand is, how can you, who don't know me or understand me, who never in your life have come into my dark little home, who haven't seen the poverty and hardship in which I live with my poor little family, how can you, who haven't seen or understood how the bullet flew or who it hit or who carries its wound, how can you, an outsider who's never even been there, hire yourself out to condemn me, to bury me, and to strew ashes on my grave because the rich man Shloyme and his wife tell you to? You're paid to do it? But Khatskl the servant was promised, by his owner, a ruble for every blow he gave me; how are you better than that brute Khatskl, Mr. Lawyer?"

The public laughed, the judge also smiled.

"I ask you, Your Honor," the lawyer turned to the judge, "tell the impudent woman to close her mouth."

The judge explained to Khyene that this is not the place to get into an argument with a lawyer over issues which do not pertain to the current matter. He then called the lawyer to speak.

The advocate began and spoke for an hour, showing from the witnesses' testimony that Khyene and her son were known thieves and that he wondered why this was the first time they stood in court. Then he set himself to show that there are many such mothers who, under the pretext of sending their children to school, actually carry out large and small robberies through these same children, just as Khyene, the accused, had done in this case.

"Your Honor," said the lawyer, "this woman had no other intent than to have her son rob the rich children, and, through her little thief's friendships with rich children, find entry into their rich mothers' homes to carry out further robberies there. This proves that this poor woman gave her child to Berl Shatz precisely so he would find himself near rich children. And one should take into account that there is a charity school, a Talmud-Torah, where poor parents don't need to pay a single kopeck to have their children taught. And considering that Jews are in general a folk who don't spend a single unnecessary groschen, one sees clearly and distinctly that Khyene's only motivation was that her child carry out more robberies through the school.

"Considering Khyene herself, one doesn't have to be very astute," the lawyer pointed out further, "to see what type of woman she is, and that court proceedings are just a game to her. The Honorable Judge mainly needs to know that among Jews there is a class of women under the name 'zogerins'—God-fearing, well-educated women who lead other women in prayer in the synagogue. The majority of these zogerins use their profession only to gain entrance to rich houses in order to steal and carry away whatever comes to hand. And it's because of them that many Jewish housewives come to court accusing their house servants of various thefts. Whereas, the truly guilty ones should be sought among the holy, well-educated zogerins. And one can certainly say that guiltless domestic servants suffer so much for the sake of such women, as the case was with the servant Khatskl, who was gratuitously abused over the business of the half ruble that Yosele had stolen from his Rebbe.

"Therefore, for a truly correct outcome, one must once and for all strongly punish Khyene, who is certainly a leader of a whole organized band of women operating under the mask of *zogerins,* so that she may serve as an example to the others!

"Also I beg the Honorable Judge to consider her intention to attack the householder and to remember that Shloyme Shmerelovitsh Ayzenharts is the richest merchant in town, a man who earns respect from everyone, and that his wife is a quiet woman who has only loving kindness and compassion for the poor, who hasn't got the heart to really punish even this thief, who obtained by cunning her only son's last morsel, as several of the witnesses here today have attested, specifically Leah Shatz, Berl the *melamed's* wife.

"I also ask the judge to take into account the insolence of said Khyene, who burst into a quiet happy home in the middle of the day, cursing and reviling esteemed people, breaking mirrors and furniture in the house, in consequence of which the worthy Mrs. Ayzenharts became sick for a few days, which even the accused woman doesn't deny. All this together gives me the right to request the harshest punishment for the accused."

"Have you anything more to say?" the judge asked Khyene as the lawyer ended his long speech.

"I have only this to say," Khyene answered. "That neither I nor my son are thieves! About everything else that prosecuting devil said I know nothing. What I have done, I have not denied, and if Your Honor finds me guilty, let him pour out the entire punishment on me alone. I'll take it all for the good, but don't judge my poor child to be a thief! No great damage will come to me, an adult, from your punishment. My consolation is: God really knows my truth! But your punishment can really harm a small child, who needs to begin living, who will perhaps soon not have a mother, who will soon have to get used to living at the mercy of other peoples' kindness. Have pity for my child, Your Honor! A forlorn mother asks righteousness and compassion for an innocent child! I don't have the strength for more; no complaint and no words."

The judge wrote and wrote. Finally the public stood and the judge read the verdict: "For the scandal and unrest in Shloyme Shmerelovitsh Ayzenharts' house, I sentence Khyene to ten days in prison. As to the guilt of her son, the sexton's son Yosl Borekhovitsh, in various small and large robberies, and of his mother Khyene, in hiding and concealing the said stolen items, I pronounce not guilty for lack of proof."

The judge got the lawyer to sign and then Khyene.

"I thank you, Your Honor," Khyene said, "I'm happy with your judgment, as long as my child is not named as a thief. I have only one more request: please let me be taken quickly, straight from here to the place where I must serve my sentence. I only hope, whether healthy or sick, to be freed and home with my husband and poor children by Rosh Hashanah!"

The judge called the policeman to take Khyene to jail.

"Go home, my child," she said to Yosele as she kissed him. "Tell your father the court itself said that you are no thief! Tell him I pray he not beat you for no reason. It will make my time in prison easier. And I ask you, my child: get used to being without your mother. Who knows, perhaps this will soon come in handy to you. Be honest, pious, and good to everybody; God, blessed be He, will see your misery!"

# TEN

A few days before Rosh Hashanah, Khyene was set free. People who had known her mother swore they thought, "There goes Rukhl the Preacher's wife, a stooped, sick Jewess, not her daughter Khyene, who was always so lively, efficient, and skillful!"

Khyene had been in prison for just ten days, but she'd aged more than ten years. Going home from the police station she had to sit down ten times to rest herself. She didn't speak a word to anyone. "She is only a shadow of the former Khyene," people said, "and it seems as though she already looks into her own grave!"

At Rosh Hashanah, Khyene sat like a stone in the synagogue; she didn't speak, she didn't read, she didn't even cry! She also didn't sit in her usual place, but sat near the door, nearer to the fresh air.

On Yom Kippur, the women said Khyene moved Heaven and earth with her crying and lamentations. And who could pay attention to the cantor or his helpers? Whoever heard Khyene's prayers to God, her pleas for her husband and children, knew the true purpose of Yom Kippur, and what it meant to plead to God with a broken heart!

And not for nothing was she pleading so fervently. Her heart told her, apparently, said the women, that this was her last Yom Kippur on earth. She said goodbye to all the women around her, asking their pardon in case she had unintentionally offended the honor of any one of them, and asking them not to abandon her little children. And as the women consoled her, saying she would tell about this misery in some future happy hour, she answered, "I shall soon tell the Living God of my children's desolation when I come to His Heavenly dwelling."

At Neilah she suddenly became black as the earth. From her throat came a torrent, a river of blood. No water, no cry, and no *"gevalt"* helped. She was half carried, half borne home by wagon before the evening prayers, and by the next day she was already lying on the ground, decked in a black cover that a sexton had brought.

Before the funeral, two candles burned near her head in her own candlesticks, and at her feet lay her sick husband and her eldest daughter, already exhausted from sobbing and lamentations. The other daughter held one of the twins by the hand; the other twin had been taken in by a neighbor.

But Yosele cried more than all of them, tore his hair, and banged his little head against the wall. "Oy, Mama, Mama," the poor child shrieked, "don't die, my dear mother, don't die! Better I should die! Oy, Mama, my Mama!"

And those who came in, cried too, hearing how the despairing child lamented for his good mother.

This didn't go on for long. The casket came. Women of the Burial Society gave Khyene her due, and she had a funeral not like an ordinary pauper. In her whole life Khyene had not been talked about around town as much as she was during those last few weeks. People spoke especially about the time from her day in court to the day of her death, and now that she was gone, everyone wanted to talk about how such an impressive orator died. And thanks to that, she had quite a nice funeral.

When she was laid in her grave, and after the third shovelful of dirt when the burial attendants had begged her forgiveness and all honor had been done to her, Borekh and the children raised such a sobbing and crying that nobody noticed how one woman sobbed over the half open grave.

"Khyene," cried the woman, "Sheyndele begs your forgiveness and asks that you be a good intercessor for her, her husband, and their only child!"

Yosele, crying, said the Kaddish by heart, speaking out each word clearly, and his tears did not stop flowing.

"Khyene didn't take on the whole world for her Yosele in vain!" said the women returning from the cemetery. "Such a Kaddish is worth it all. Really her troubles shall be laid to rest, God in Heaven, and her Kaddish-sayer will be a thief no more!"

The menfolk discussed what should now be done with Borekh the Sexton, with his two little children whose mother had weaned them only a half-year ago. If one could find a childless couple to take the children and raise them as their own, it would be a true salvation. Unfortunately, the town was blessed by God, and there were no childless couples to be found.

People talked and talked and came to the conclusion that Borekh and his two infants were truly the town's burden and it simply wasn't known what kind of advice to give.

During Borekh's few days of sitting shivah, he and his children were not lacking for bread. Jews aren't stingy when it comes to an inexpensive mitzvah, and the neighbors brought bagels and eggs to the funeral feast, enough for him and his little brood for that day and the next. People even envied Borekh's luck: that he didn't have to sit shivah more than three days in all because "the holiday takes precedence."

Old heads of households who never forgot that Borekh had been their sexton, remembered at this time to hold back a bit of the extra fees from the current sexton and save the money for Borekh. Others sent challah, meat, and potatoes, so the holiday would not be spoiled for Borekh and his family.

Every day, morning and evening, Yosele went to the study house to say Kaddish. As long as he was a new little orphan by the cantor's pulpit, the wound in his heart still fresh and his little voice like his eyes, full of tears, nobody reminded him that he was a thief. However, the holiday was barely past before people became used to his Kaddish, and with nobody to stand up for him, the older Kaddish-sayers began to drive him from the podium, and he began to hear the words again, "Thief! Yosele, thief, go to court to say Kaddish!"

At home, things were also growing worse each day. The eldest daughter was not able to provide enough food for everyone from the five guldens a week Borekh received from the occasional neighbor. Khyene's four candlesticks were already sold, her few cushions already bought by the neighbors, and the family had already eaten up all the money. The owner of the apartment where Borekh lived had already promised it to another. When Borekh was feeling the whole pack of troubles his wife had left him, he let out all his anger on Yosele, whom he considered to be at fault for all the unhappiness that had come to him. The poor child had, in addition to hunger, no lack of curses and blows.

Only Yoyne the Water Carrier hadn't turned his loving kindness away from Borekh and his household. In addition to the free bucket of water he had begun to bring unfailingly every day since Khyene's death, he spared no effort to plan with the poor family, so they wouldn't, God forbid, die in a day from hunger, the poor things.

Once Yoyne came late in the evening, exhausted, and said after he wiped the sweat away with the hem of his garment,

"Long life to Jews, may God help them! True, it took me quite a bit of effort before I succeeded, but because I'm Yoyne, I spoke out as one must if one has to speak to a rich man, really grab him. I've talked and talked to the caretaker at the Visiting the Sick Society until the sweat was pouring off me. But I have properly prevailed! And I've got a certificate, and you will be taken into the poorhouse. I've even seen your bed already—if only my bed at home were as good! There's food there, and a doctor, and medicine, and if God, blessed be He, wills it, you will recover from your cough there.

"I don't have any worries about your girls. Getsl the Women's Tailor wants to take your Sorele, and he'll even give her shoes and a dress. I'll also find a place for your Rukhele; until then, she can stay with me. My wife has undertaken to pluck forty pounds of feathers for a rich bride, so Rukhl will earn her bread properly by helping her.

"I'll put Yosele in the Talmud-Torah, and I'll find sponsors to pay for his daily meals if he's good and studies well. If not, I can't put my head on his shoulders. In the worst case, I'll give him to a tradesman—a tradesman who is a pious Jew, Reb Borekh.

"My greatest worry was for your twins, may they both prosper. A plan came to me that Simkha the Nobleman's Land Manager, a man without sons, would be coming in from out of town for a yortzeit. Why shouldn't such a rich man take the poor little orphans and raise them as his own?

"Praise God, said and done! Simkha came, prayed, said Kaddish, gave a handsome donation for a passage of Mishnah that had been learned in his father's honor. Really very lovely. So I said to Simkha in front of the whole congregation, 'You perform the mitzvah of honoring one's father to the maximum, and for this may God grant you long life. But a man should consider while he's still alive, 'What will come of me after a hundred and twenty years? Who will say Kaddish for me, who will learn a passage of Mishnah for me?'

"Simkha gave a bitter sigh and asked, 'How am I guilty that God has punished me so?'

"'Don't sigh, Reb Simkha!' I consoled him. 'You aren't guilty. God, blessed be He, has helped you! You can save children, put them in school, raise them as good Jews; they'll learn God's Torah. It's just that he didn't give you your own children. On the other hand, God gave an affliction to another, gave him children, beautiful children, brilliant children, but then took their mother from them before her time, before she was able to stand them on their feet, and their father is sick, can barely keep body and soul together, and is thanking God for the mercy that he'll be taken into the poorhouse, may it never happen to you. So I ask you, what need is there to sigh that you don't have your own children, while here such dear twin boys are homeless and could die from hunger at any time? You could take them for your own and put them in school, and after one hundred and twenty years, it's they who'll be saying Kaddish for you and reciting the Mishnah passage.'

"Everyone was silent. 'Why are you quiet, Jews?' I shouted, 'I've had my say, now have yours! Talk costs nothing, why are you silent?' So people talked and talked, and Simkha decided to take one child. 'That won't do!' I called out. 'The God who helps with salt will help with pepper, too! The God who helps you as you take one orphan will help you with the other, to raise them to Torah, to the chuppah, and to good deeds! If you can take both, that's good. If not, simpler not to take either.'

"In short, Reb Borekh, I prevailed. Simkha and his wife are coming tomorrow. And if the Master of the Universe wills it, your children will grow up with them, with all good things! Nu, Reb Borekh, aren't I right when I say Jews are really a good folk, may God help them!"

The two older girls cried quietly at the end to which Borekh was making of Mama's family. But what else was left for them to do?

Simkha and his wife, Perele, a corpulent woman in expensive clothes, did in fact come in the morning. Yoyne brought them around to Borekh; they looked the children over and found them emaciated, meager, but suitably beautiful, happy children. Perele cried looking at them, at their poor cradle, and even poorer bedclothes.

She kissed them and with tears in her eyes gave one to her husband. The other she took in her own arms and said: "Your pious mama, who couldn't live to see pleasure and delight from you, will, in her holy rest, be a good intercessor for me and for my husband, that we will be able to raise you up to Torah and the chuppah and to do righteous good deeds! She shall pray there Above, that your real father, sisters, and brother shall live to experience great joys with you, equally with me and my husband!"

Neighbors, men and women, wished Simkha and his wife a "mazl tov" and all that is good. Simkha brought out gingerbread and brandy and Perele gave cheese and butter to Yosele and his sisters. They left a couple of rubles for Borekh, and then rode off with the twins. Yoyne got a bit drunk from the celebration, and taking his yoke and two water pails, he shouted all day long, "Jews are really a good folk, may God help them!"

# Eleven

A few days later, Borekh was already in the poorhouse, lying on his cot, as Yoyne had said, like a king, Sorele had gone back to Getsl the Women's Tailor. Rukhl was staying meanwhile with Yoyne, helping his wife pluck feathers, and it was only Yosele who wasn't taken care of. He could go to the poor boys' school, but what about his food?

In vain, Yoyne the Water Carrier ran around asking the householders to whom he brought water if they would pledge to feed Yosele one day in the week; not one of them was willing. "Khyene's boy has such a terrible reputation," they answered. "His mother went to prison because of him. It's because of him she's dead and her family is in ruins, and according to what is said, he really is a thief who simply tears things from your hands. How can one let someone like that into one's home, or even into one's kitchen, where it isn't possible to watch him closely enough to keep him from stealing?"

In vain, Yoyne swore it was all a lie spread across the town by Sheyndele the Tax Assessor's wife, may her name be erased. "Yosele is a good boy. He can study and he wants to study, and one will earn the World to Come if one gives him one day of food a week."

"Don't swear, Yoyne," he was answered. "These days one can't even swear for one's own children, let alone another's child who's already been in court! 'Where there's smoke, there's fire!'"

Yoyne saw he had no choice. He went to Hershl the Shoe-maker, who although a shoemaker, was a pious Jew and a good craftsman. But Hershl demanded a contract stating that Yosele would work for free until he was fifteen years old, and thereafter would work three years more at fifty rubles a year. Such an agreement, however, Borekh didn't want to sign.

"You know, Reb Yoyne," said Borekh, "Khyene's whole desire was that Yosele be a scholar. And why should I lie to you? That was also my desire, always, although I vexed her about it, may she forgive me. But I don't want to give him away to a shoemaker because I know Yosele has a fiery mind for learning. He has an iron memory, and a sharp understanding—no evil eye. In good hands, he could turn out to be a distinguished scholar. Therefore, in order that your good deed be complete, give him meanwhile to a craftsman so he has a place to spend the winter. And in the summer, if God helps, send him to Vilna, where his uncle lives, one of Khyene's brothers, a distinguished scholar. He'll study with him."

The plan pleased Yoyne, and he again spoke with the craftsman, asking him to take Yosele without a contract. But Hershl didn't want this, so Yoyne gave Yosele away to Zeligl, a fine young man, a shoemaker, who at times had a love for drink. Yoyne even knew this, but what would it matter to Yosele? "Let him drink to his heart's desire," Yoyne said, "as long as Yosele has a place to lay his head until summer and won't have to drag himself around hungry in the streets."

It wasn't so easy for Yoyne to talk Yosele into this, going to Zeligl's to become a shoemaker. "Mama will come choke me!" the child lamented and cried. "I should study. Put me in a cheder, I won't even cry if the Rebbe beats me, just don't give me away to a shoemaker!"

However, his laments and tears were of no use. Yoyne was himself a man burdened with many little children, and was a pauper to boot, and so Yosele had no choice and was away to the shoemaker.

For two weeks Yosele wandered like a dog while living with his new master, the fine fellow. He did many awful jobs for him, as the Jews did for the Pharaoh's overseers: he carried water and wood, polished boots, "gathered" kindling for his master from other people's yards, and slaved for every worker in the shop, and never heard his actual name, "Yosele."

All he ever heard from Zeligl was "Thief, bastard, the devil take your father! Thief, buy me a gulden's worth of brandy! Crook, bring tar! Robber, lay out the nails! Swindler, bring my thread, a plague on your head!"

Once Yosele was grabbed as he was dragging a basket of kindling from someone else's yard, as Zeligl had sent him to do. The kindling was taken from him and his bones were well broken.

Yosele returned, badly beaten, with an empty basket, so Zeligl laid a few more good blows on him and shouted, "Thief, who told you to steal? I told you to *gather!*"

"I did gather," Yosele said, "as I do every day."

"That's a lie, you stole!" Zeligl yelled. "You think gathering is stealing?"

Yosele didn't know the difference between gathering and stealing, and when his master sent him the next day to gather once again with the basket, he answered: "Gathering is also stealing. I don't want to be a thief!" At this, the master beat him murderously and gave him nothing to eat for a whole day.

Another time, when Yosele was coming back from evening prayers, the master called out to him in such a friendly way, the outcast child didn't believe Zeligl meant him. "Yosele, do you want a sour pickle?" asked the master.

Yosele was afraid to answer. He'd been fooled a few times this way, and when he'd answered, "Yes," he was answered with a coarse word as the master and his journeymen laughed.

"Word of honor, a pickle, a sour one!" the master swore. "I'm not fooling this time, no, really, a pickle. Tell me, do you want it?"

"I do!" Yosele answered, thanks to what the master had said.

"Here, take this cup, crawl in through the window in this cellar. There, in the right-hand corner, stands a barrel of pickles. Take a full cup. I'll stand by the window and you can hand them to me! Show your handicraft. You're very clever with your finger work."

"It's forbidden to steal!" Yosele answered.

"Thief, who are you talking to?" Zeligl shouted. "And I suppose it's all right to steal money from a Rebbe? A pocketknife from school? A spoon from Sheyndele's kitchen? That's okay? Have you lost your senses? Do you think I don't know who you are?"

Yosele was afraid to answer and stood silent.

"Are you going in or not?" asked Zeligl. "Is it beneath your dignity?"

"I don't want a pickle," Yosele said, avoiding the question. Zeligl kicked him with his foot. "Do you want this? And do you want a plague, a blow? Such a thief, God forbid, one should ask him to go into a Jewish house?"

Another boy volunteered, and a few minutes later, the master and his journeymen were all eating sour pickles and bread. Because of his stubbornness, Yosele didn't even get a dry crust of bread to eat.

From that day on, the business with the cellar was repeated every night. Every night they drew straws: who would creep into the cellar? They made it so that Yosele drew that straw each time. Yosele, however, shouted every time that he didn't want any pickles, and the master called another boy to go instead, after first hitting Yosele three times, which each boy administered with one additional punch as his own "justice."

It wasn't just pickles lifted from the cellar, but also cider-apples, onions, potatoes, and everything a well-to-do housewife laid by for a whole winter. Nobody ever gave Yosele anything from these heists.

Once the master decreed, "Tomorrow, if the thief won't take a basket of potatoes and all the other good things from that cellar, you all hear me, as I'm a Jew, I will drive him out like a dog. I hate a goody-goody. If it's good enough for us, it must be good enough for the little thief! A downfall to him! It's really just stubbornness! Look here, thief, if one can steal for a mother, one may steal for one's master. You're a thief in any case. If you don't want to obey me, and go where I send you, when will you obey me? Remember, thief, tomorrow is your day of judgment! Either I'll drive you out, or you'll remain a thief!"

That night, Yosele had a dream: he saw his mother, she was so pale, so emaciated that his heart hurt looking at her. "See, my dear child," she begged him, "don't be a thief, don't steal pickles, look at me and see what happened to me because of you, to sit in prison and become so sick! You should want to learn, Yosele. The Torah will protect you from all evil. Don't be a shoemaker! My ancestors were not shoemakers, so how have you come to this?"

He wanted to answer her. He wanted to sob himself out for her, his heart was so bitter and heavy! Suddenly, he remembered that his mother was actually dead, and with a cry of anguish he begged her, "Oy Mama, don't choke me, I won't be a shoemaker!"

And there he glimpsed, under her red shawl, her white shroud. She raised up her dried-out dead arms and said, "Don't be afraid, I'm not dead!"

"Yes, you are dead, I say Kaddish for you!" he cried with anguish.

"Good, good, my child, say Kaddish often, often, I'll petition God for you!" she consoled him. Then he saw her rise up. She didn't walk, but floated and drifted into the air, high above the fence, and then farther away to the cemetery. He screamed with anguish, "Mama, Mama!" But although he screamed with his last strength, he couldn't hear his own voice.

The boys who were lying in a heap with him on the floor, sleeping—if you could call it that—heard his muffled cry of anguish and woke him up. "What did you dream, thief?" one of them asked. "You screamed with such a voice, I thought bandits were falling on us to slaughter us."

"Those in the Other World were smiting his soul for his sins," another shoemaker's apprentice explained. "Everyone's soul flies to Heaven at night, but a wicked man flies straight into Gehennah and gets some fiery lashes."

It was still some time before dawn and the others quickly went back to sleep, but Yosele couldn't sleep any more. He could only think with terror of his dream, and that his upcoming "Day of Judgment," as the master had called it, was here. He couldn't stop thinking about it.

When the clock struck six the master woke all his apprentices with a kick in the side, and Yosele, too, got up and was away to the study house to pray and say Kaddish. And on this day he recited many, many Kaddishes. It seemed somehow to him that his mother was in the women's shul. She heard his Kaddish and answered, "Amen," and winked at him, indicating that he should wait and not go out yet. He stayed through the second prayer minyan and said Kaddish again. He then prayed with the third minyan and said all the Kaddishes.

Finally the whole congregation was gone, and he left, too. But he stood like a stone by the doorstep, and it suddenly occurred to him with chagrin: why couldn't one pray for an entire day? If one prayed all day, he thought to himself, one could say a hundred Kaddishes! To stay here all day, and not have to go back to the master! Remembering the master gave him a sting in his little heart, and he remembered that the master would soon give it to him good—would kill him for staying so long at his prayers. The apprentices had long since eaten everything up, he thought and wondered, "What reason will I give him for coming so late from praying?"

Then he said to himself, "No, I won't go to the master any more," and began to walk quickly, not knowing where he was going. He wandered for a couple of hours until he began to get hungry. But the hungrier he got the quicker he walked until he arrived at the bank of the river where he had so often gone with the Rebbetzin and her laundry.

Heading to the water, he stretched out to his full length and began to drink, although he didn't want to drink at all. He thought perhaps water might satisfy his hunger since he had no food. He somehow thought he never wanted to eat again as he started back to town.

In the marketplace, he scrounged up a couple of half-eaten apples, and there, where the women sit with all kinds of vegetables, he found a withered, unclaimed pickle and half a carrot. He picked it up, wiped the mud off, and ate it with appetite. He felt strengthened and remembered it was time for prayers and the saying of Kaddish. In the study house he forgot everything else, prayed Mincha by heart, said Kaddish, and remained until after evening prayers.

Jealously, and with a grieving little heart, he saw how each of the older yeshiva boys took a candle, stood by the table, opened a Gemara, and studied.

He wanted such happiness for himself, so he went to the bookshelf to find a Khumesh.

"What are you looking for, young man?" someone asked.

"A Khumesh!"

"Why do you need a Khumesh?"

"I want to study!"

"Don't you have a school?"

"No!"

"Who are you?"

"Yosele!"

"What are you saying to him?" a schoolboy broke in as he came to the bookshelf. "This is that little thief. Not long ago he was in court. If he gets a chance he'll steal a prayer book!"

"Is it true, boy?" the man asked.

"I don't want to steal, I want to study!" Yosele answered. "If you'll give me a Khumesh, I'll study."

"Here's a Khumesh," the man said. "I'll see if you can study and if that's what you really want. Come, sit here by me."

And with cheer and pleasure, Yosele studied Khumesh before the Jew, who didn't need to help him at all.

"You're a fine lad!" the man said, "but tell me, since you can study so well, why do people call you a thief?"

Yosele didn't answer, but tears showed in his little eyes.

"Did you ever steal?" the man asked.

"I won't any more, never again!" answered the beaten-down boy.

"If you don't steal any more, if you'll just study, you'll be a respectable person!" the man consoled him. But the man never asked, "Have you eaten today? Do you have somewhere to sleep?" The man forgot, or it never occurred to him, that this child had had nothing to eat and didn't even have a home.

Nevertheless, for as long as the man stayed in the study house, nobody touched Yosele. But barely had his protector departed when the sexton, who had always been angry at Yosele's father because of the five guldens that had been taken from him for Borekh's sake, grabbed the Khumesh away from Yosele, snuffed out the candle, and drove him away.

"Go home, you rascal!" he shouted.

Where was his home? That wasn't the sexton's problem.

Tired from wandering the whole day, Yosele crept into a little corner in the big study house vestibule. He laid himself down and slept the whole night through until men came in to pray with the first minyan.

And again he managed to scrounge up the day's food: a rotten, gnawed-over apple, a little carrot, and other such discarded things which only he would eat—if he could take it into his mouth, he had no complaint. And there was no lack of water in the river. On this same day, another happiness befell him: a woman gave him a kopeck to help drag her wet laundry home from the river. With his kopeck he bought bread, and was, on this day, completely full.

But his protector from yesterday didn't come to evening prayers, and so nobody gave him a Khumesh for studying. The sexton drove him out again, but this time suggested compassionately that he go to the Chassidic study house, where people didn't know him and would let him lay down his head.

Yosele went to the Chassidic study house. It was dark and only one candle burned on the lectern. There were no yeshiva boys, so there were also no holy books. The sexton, an old, half-blind Jew, didn't notice at all that there was anyone else there besides him, and Yosele crept near the oven and slept like a prince.

On the third day, Yoyne the Water Carrier grabbed him by the river. He twisted his ears violently and yelled: "Rascal, I took so much trouble over you, just to have you creep into somebody else's cellar to steal pickles! You really are, truly, a thief. When the world says, 'Thief,' one should believe it. Even Zeligl drove you out. So much for my good deed!"

"It wasn't me who stole pickles from the cellar," Yosele swore. "I didn't want to go and that's why the master beat me. As I am a Jew, it wasn't me!"

"Then come to the master, let me hear both sides, eye to eye," Yoyne said.

"I'm afraid he'll kill me! I don't want to be a shoemaker. I want to study in the *besmedresh*, the way everyone studies!"

"Where do you eat? Where do you sleep?"

Yosele didn't know what to answer.

"Go back to the master, ask his forgiveness, ask him to just take you back. If not, you'll become a vagabond dragging yourself from place to place. If you haven't yet become a thief, you'll have to become one. Go, I'm telling you!" Yoyne shouted.

"I don't want to be a shoemaker and I won't go back to Zeligl, even if you kill me!" Yosele answered decisively.

"Are you really such a rascal that you won't obey me? Then go to hell. What you brew, that's what you'll drink! God is my witness, I've done what I can." Yoyne leaned down to pick up his yoke and pails of water, but Yosele thought he meant to hit him and ran away. Yoyne called out after him, "Just as the world says: a no-goodnik! What a rascal, what a bum!"

Thus, did the forsaken child spend several days with nothing to worry about. He and hunger were already old acquaintances. He slept no worse in the vestibule or next to the oven in the Chassidic house of prayer than he did on the ground at Zeligl's.

Only one thing made his life bitter and always brought tears to his eyes: meeting up with boys going to or coming from cheder. "All the boys go," his little heart cried out in him. "They have a place to go. They have a cheder, a Rebbe, and a home! But I have nothing. I go around in the streets, I don't study, and I also have no home!" And how he envied those boys. And how he used to pray to God that he would again have a cheder and a Rebbe, even a Rebbe that beat him. But Yosele no longer prayed for a home. How could he have a home when he no longer had a mother?

Once, passing by a cheder where a modern Rebbe from Vilna was holding forth with his students, he overheard the Rebbe teaching passages to the children with a lovely tune. He couldn't tear himself away, and stood under the window, listening to what was being taught. From then on, he went back every day to stand for hours near the window. His heart melted. He devoured the Rebbe's every word until the children came outside, saw him, and drove him away with the cry, "Thief, thief!"

One day, he met up with his sister, Sorele, who hadn't yet heard that he had run away from Zeligl the Shoemaker. When Yosele told her, she began to cry.

"Don't cry," he consoled her, "I won't be a shoemaker. In a dream Mama begged me not to be a shoemaker. She wanted me to study. And now I'm learning, Sorele. I'm learning so well, even better than when I was with Reb Berl!"

"Where are you studying?"

"Come, I'll show you," he answered happily, and he took his sister to the window. "Can you hear, Sorele? Here one can learn better and more nicely than at Reb Berl's! Here's where I sit every day and study just like all the other boys," he told his sister joyously. "Ask me something, you'll see that I know

it all, everything they're learning here in the cheder!" And he
began reciting by heart the passage with the same beautiful
melody he'd heard under the window.

"Where do you live? Where do you sleep?" Sorele asked,
crying.

"In the Chassidic prayer house," he answered. "The sexton
there is better than in our study house. He doesn't chase me away
like the other one does—the one who wouldn't even give me a
Khumesh."

"And where do you eat, what do you eat, my poor Yosele?"
she asked further. As before, Yosele didn't know how to answer.
He remained silent, but tears appeared in his little eyes.

"Come with me, my dear Yosele, I'll share my last bite with
you!" his good sister said, sobbing. "Come, don't be afraid. My
mistress won't do anything to me if I give you half of my lunch
and dinner!"

And she took him home with her, to share her little bit with
him. Reb Getsl the Women's Tailor was pleased that Sorele had
such a good heart. "Pity the poor child!" he said, and he didn't
say a word against Sorele when she put away half of her breakfast
and lunch for her little brother every day.

She bought him a shirt and a pair of socks from the few
groschen that came to her from the deliveries she made. His
good mother had provided him with shoes before her death.
Sorele combed his hair and washed him. When she gave him
his portion of breakfast, Yosele was truly happy—happy, because
nobody was beating him, and even happier that he was studying,
even if only in the street under a window somewhere. The days
were still warm enough, the window was almost always open,
and he clearly heard and grasped every word the Rebbe taught.
He remembered the beautiful melody very well, and all the

translations, and he sometimes wanted to prompt the boys who forgot a word or didn't know what it meant. Neither the boys' insults nor their spitting on him through the window could drive him from the beloved little spot that God had sent him. He had all he wanted now!

Once a boy from the school, either accidentally or on purpose, poured hot tea out the window on him, and Yosele let out an agonizing cry. The teacher ran outside and brought him into the school. Luckily the tea wasn't dangerously hot and no blisters rose on his skin.

"Little boy, who are you? What are you doing here?" the teacher asked.

"I'm learning here!" Yosele answered innocently.

"What? Where? Here in the street?"

"My Mama is dead!" the child explained. "I have no cheder. I hear everything you are studying with your boys from under the window."

The teacher was curious. "Nu, then tell me, exactly what do you know after such learning?" Yosele began repeating everything by heart that he had overheard through the window.

The teacher marveled, shrugged his shoulders, patted the poor child on his head, and was willing to let him come study every day inside the school. However, his students and the mistress of the school told him this boy—who seemed like such an unfortunate creature—was actually a known thief, and that for his sake, Reb Berl had almost lost his entire cheder. They insisted it was not appropriate to let such a fellow into the school. Consequently, the compassionate teacher told Yosele he could sit under the window every day, as much as he liked, but he must swear, on his share of the World to Come, never to steal from the boys.

He also explained to the schoolboys how grave a sin it was to tease and insult a poor boy, an orphan who had no mother to put him into a school, even though he was able to learn and wanted to learn. Moreover, it's a good deed to help him however one can and not to begrudge him an occasional piece of bread through the window instead of spitting on him!

From that day on, the schoolboys began to have pity on Yosele, and often one of them would offer him a piece of bread with butter through the window or a half-eaten bagel left over from breakfast, and Yosele's eyes became happier.

He also had somewhere to go at night. In exchange for sweeping the floor in the early mornings and pouring water into the basins, the old sexton of the Chassidic prayer house let him sleep for free near the oven every night. He always prayed in the *besmedresh*. He once tried to pray with the Chassids, but when someone prompted him to say, "Our salvation will grow" during the Kaddish, he didn't say it. A fervent Chassid took him by the ear and muttered that if he were ever so impertinent again to not include this phrase in the Kaddish, he'd never be allowed back in the prayer house.

Yosele hated this phrase—although he himself didn't know why—and wouldn't recite it. So it was better that every morning and by night he would run to the *besmedresh* to pray and say Kaddish. He sometimes got a Khumesh at the *besmedresh*, and could review what he had learned from his father and from Reb Berl.

And how happy he was when, seeking a Khumesh on one occasion, he'd opened a different holy book and found the chapters in Isaiah which he'd memorized under the window at the Vilna Rebbe's school! Now he saw in print what he had learned by ear. He so loved the letters and the words—they were so dear to him—his eyes lit up completely and he read over the chapters several times.

"Little boy," a man asked him, seeing how he studied so diligently. "Do you already know the entire *Svarbe?*"

Yosele didn't yet know that the book from which he was studying was called a *"Svarbe"* and contained the twenty-four books of the Hebrew Bible. He only remembered that his Rebbe, Reb Berl, once said they would study *Svarbe* together the following semester. He now undertook to ask his sister Sorele to buy a *Svarbe* for him so he could study it every night, even in the Chassidic prayer house.

But here a misfortune occurred. Suddenly, at Getsl the Women's Tailor's, an expensive accessory was lost from a rich woman's dress, and the suspicion fell on Yosele. In vain, Sorele cried and swore that neither she nor her forlorn brother knew anything about the robbery, but Getsl answered her, "You are really an honest child. I would swear for *you* myself, but I won't vouch for your little brother! When the world accuses, there must be something to it. But why should I suspect him? If he's not guilty, I've sinned, and what good is that to me? Better he shouldn't come here, then I won't suspect him. If you want to give him some of your food, I've got no quarrel with that! But give it to him some time during the week. Work it out so he never comes here again. Understand?"

When Yosele arrived, Sorele cried. She asked him to come to her only on Shabbes because the master wouldn't tolerate his presence. She would figure out how to give him his portion of her food. "If Yoyne the Water Carrier didn't live so far away, I would leave something for you every day at his house. Meanwhile, take a few kopecks so you can buy yourself something. Go, my poor little brother! Our mother's merits will protect you, and God will send me advice about how to keep you from going hungry all day!"

"Buy me a *Svarbe*, Sorele!" he asked her, sobbing. "Yesterday the window was already closed at school, and I could hear nothing of what the Rebbe was teaching. If I had a *Svarbe*, I could study by myself at night in the prayer house. *Svarbe*, Sorele, is such a good thing, all I want to do is study *Svarbe* all day."

Sorele promised him she would scrounge up enough money for a *Svarbe*. Downhearted, Yosele left for the cheder, but when he got there, he saw the window had already been closed. They were putting in the double shutters and stopping up all the cracks. He heard the teaching going on inside, but only a voice with no words, and he realized he no longer had a place to study.

He sat for a long time under the window, but finally got up and walked away. And his little heart pained him as he said goodbye to the precious little spot that had become so beloved to him.

# Twelve

The next day the autumn rains began in earnest, bringing the deep, thick autumn mud and the cold gray days with dark nights that make one tremble, and things became truly grim for the shivering child. During the night he could stay in the Chassidic prayer house, but in the morning, soon after morning prayers, the schoolboys and the sexton always drove him away from the *besmedresh*. The sexton locked the doors and went off somewhere to be by himself, and Yosele had no choice but to wander around through the muddy streets, soaked by the rain, until Mincha arrived, and he could freely enter the *besmedresh* again.

He survived this way for a couple of days, but on the third day, he noticed there was not enough left from his few kopecks to buy bread. For over an hour, he stood shivering under the edge of a roof hiding from the rain, his little heart fainting. It was already past noon, and he had not had a bit of food in his mouth all morning. He couldn't remember the exact accounting of his coins and tried to search again in his pockets in case there was a missing kopeck. He sought, groped, nothing.

He remembered: somewhere in the world there was a market where he once found things to keep himself going. And despite the rain and mud he set off for the marketplace, but found the whole plaza abandoned and empty.

He remembered the meaning of the words, "*toyu vovoyu,*" the world as God first created it, "formless and void." He said to himself, "That's exactly the way this market looks. There's so much water you can't even see the mud. Muddy water 'on the surface of the abyss!'"

No women with fruit, no peasants with wagons. Instead of a little piece of already bitten apple, instead of a little piece of carrot, which would have been so delightful to him now, he saw only a river of water with bubbles endlessly swirling and disappearing.

It occurred to him to try and count the bubbles, and he forgot for a while his hunger, which was the reason he had come here in the first place. He counted and counted, and it seemed to him that these were not ordinary bubbles, but some kind of eyes that were looking at him. "Maybe they're actually spirits," he thought. "Here one lives, here one dies."

Meanwhile, it rained harder and suddenly the bubbles were all gone. He thought, "All the little souls are extinguished; flown up to Heaven. God has called them home!" But he couldn't think about this long because the water was already creeping up into his little shoes, and the rain was soaking through his clothes to his skin. He shivered and began to run. But where was he going? He himself didn't know, but for some reason he was drawn to the *besmedresh*.

Suddenly, he found himself in the vestibule. He saw the sexton and wanted to flee, but today the sexton was so good to him. Instead of driving him away, he gave him a broom to clean the mud from his little feet, and told him to come in and dry off by the oven.

He was made so happy by the sexton's kindness that he completely forgot his hunger. He sat near the oven warming himself until men arrived to pray Mincha. Between Mincha and Maariv, he took a little nap, but someone banged on the bimah and the "He is compassionate" prayer was said. He awoke, prayed Maariv, said Kaddish. The *besmedresh* emptied and the schoolboys closed their Gemaras.

Hunger began to torment Yosele. He yearned to have something to eat as he set off for his night lodging at the Chassidic prayer house.

Passing by a low, poor hut, he saw through the window a mother and her children sitting around the table eating supper. It made him think of his own mother, and he envied all children who had a mother, a home, and a supper. His mood grew bitter and he couldn't go any farther. He stood there looking through the window for quite a while.

"If only I had just one piece of bread" he thought, and the hunger gave him the courage to go in and beg for a bit of bread—something he had never tried before.

The woman gathered the remaining bits of food from the table and gave them to him. He gave her a touching look and joyously ran away without saying a word.

He took a few bites as he headed to the river. He remembered his father once told him, "One can eat a tiny portion before washing." As he ran to the Chassidic prayer house, he told himself, "I'll wash myself at the prayer house."

When he got there, he washed and ate up all the scraps, but he was still not full. He put his head under the faucet and drank, then said the blessing of bread, read the *Shema Yisroel,* and lay down to sleep.

When the sexton woke him before dawn to sweep the study house, his head ached so much he could hardly open his eyes and stand up. The sexton was barely out of sight when he laid back down and slept again. At his second waking, it took all his strength to come to his senses and stand up. His bones ached the whole day, and he had never felt so cold before.

Again, he dragged himself around in the mud, and again he went to the *besmedresh*, prayed Mincha and said Kaddish, prayed Maariv and said Kaddish again, but his little voice shook and broke, and he had to stop after every few words to catch his breath. He felt sick. "But that's because I haven't eaten anything today," he thought. "If I eat something I'll feel healthy," he consoled himself. It occurred to him to go once again to the little hut where he received the bit of bread on the previous night.

But today it wasn't hunger that drove him there. He hadn't felt hungry all day. He just wanted to ask for a bit of bread to help him feel better—so his teeth wouldn't chatter and his limbs wouldn't tremble from the cold.

"Every day to me, boy?" the woman greeted him. "I'm not the only one in town! I thank God I have enough for my own children! Last night you came to me. Today, boy, go to someone else!"

Yosele already felt regret and wanted to go out without his "cure," but the woman took him by the hand and said, "Come, I'll show you where to go." He obeyed her and followed her straight into someone else's kitchen.

The room was so light and warm. "If I could warm myself here and sleep soundly," he thought, "I'd soon be healthy." But there was nobody in the kitchen and he remained standing like a stone by the door.

Soon the cook came in and was frightened. There were silver spoons on the table. "How do you come to be in here?" she asked, counting the silver.

"Through here!" Yosele answered, pointing to the door.

"A pox on Khatskl," the cook cursed, "he leaves the silver on the table and goes away. Have you taken something already, boy?"

"I took nothing," Yosele answered. "I warmed myself a bit so I can become healthy. I'll leave soon. I don't even want a bit of bread."

During the conversation, Khatskl came in. Unknowingly, Yosele had come into Sheyndele's kitchen. Khatskl soon remembered him.

"See who you're talking to!" he shouted at the cook. "This is the thief! What is he doing here? He's come to take something into his paws, may his name be erased!"

As he spoke, he pulled Yosele toward him. "Speak, bastard, what are you doing here? Have you forgotten the blows I once gave you? Here, take this," he shouted as he hit the boy. "And remember, there is a Khatskl in this world who will make a corpse of you if your foot ever crosses this threshold again!"

"Don't beat him, Khatskl, may God beat *you!*" the cook shouted. "How can you have the heart to hit such a sick child?"

But Khatskl didn't stop. "He'll know next time!" he hollered. "Luckily, I'm just as afraid of the living Sheyndele as I am of the boy's dead mother! One is allowed to beat a thief!"

"But he hasn't stolen anything," the cook complained. "Let him be. A sick child—I wish my enemies had his health!"

"First shake him down, see if he's taken anything," Khatskl demanded. "Then, to the devil with him!"

And Khatskl shook Yosele and looked in his pockets, but didn't find anything. "Lucky for you, bastard, that you didn't have time to take anything yet. I wouldn't have left you alive! Now get lost! And warn your great-grandchildren not to fall into Khatskl's hands!"

With these words, Khatskl opened the door, and with a few more blows to his side and back, he flung the bewildered, half-dead child down the steps.

For quite a while Yosele remained lying in the street, not knowing or feeling what had happened to him. Finally, the cook, who was curious to see if he had the strength to go home, went outside to help him get up.

Yosele tried to take a few steps, but his little legs buckled under him. With his last strength, he barely dragged himself to the gate. There he sat down to rest a bit, but he soon forgot where he was. Fiery wheels, like Ezekiel's, twisted in front of his eyes, and it seemed so dark around him. Yet in the darkness, he saw some sort of people: strange, tall people with three noses and many heads. They resembled Khatskl and Sheyndele and were wild and tall as the heavens. They terrified him and he shivered. They wanted to hit him, but all at once his mother was standing before him. She cried. She stroked his head. She put him to bed and cuddled with him. Then his mother was gone and Sorele was standing near him. She handed him a *Svarbe*, an expensive *Svarbe* with big red letters that seemed to dance and jump. Suddenly he heard his father's coughing, but somehow he knew it was not his father, but he himself who was coughing. And with each cough, he felt a pain in his side. He groped with his hands to feel what hurt him so? He heard himself groan. Each breath was so heavy and he groaned again and again until he finally fell asleep.

It poured rain the whole night. No living person was out in the street. At dawn, when Reb Shoyel the Butcher was going to the slaughterhouse with his knives in one hand and his big lantern in the other, he found Yosele lying in his path. In general, Shoyel was not a coward, but he jumped back in terror when he came closer and saw the child groaning on the ground.

"What can this be? What does it signify?" Reb Shoyel asked himself. "On such a night, when not even a dog is on the street, how did this happen? Something is wrong." He carried the lantern closer.

"A Jewish child, by my word!" he exclaimed. "What is this? No! One is forbidden to pass such a thing by. I must find out quickly!"

Reb Shoyel bent over and touched the boy. "A curious thing," he said. "A warm little head. I thought he'd be frozen, but he's hot as fire." Shoyel began to wake him. "Stand up, little boy," he said raising up his little head.

Yosele opened his eyes. "Oy, my side!" he groaned.

"Who are you, little boy? Speak up, who are you?" Shoyel asked a few times until he'd roused him.

"Yosele!" the poor child barely whispered out.

"Which Yosele?" Shoyel asked.

"The thief."

"The thief? Yosele, Khyene's son of course."

"My mother was just here," the child moaned.

"Your mother is dead, silly boy. That's why you're wandering the streets." Shoyel said as if to himself. "Now tell me, why were you so foolish as to lie down to sleep in such a pouring rain? Why didn't you go home? I saw you leave last night after Maariv and believed you were going home."

"I don't have a home!" Yosele barely whispered.

"You're really not smart at all! I thought you were a clever boy. Silly thing, if you had come to me last night, I would not have driven you out. How can one spend such a cold and rainy night in the street? It's really a deathly danger!"

Yosele didn't answer. The cold was piercing him and Reb Shoyel heard how his teeth chattered in his mouth.

"Look," Shoyel said with compassion, "you've already caught cold! Come with me, I'll take you into a house. No Jew will drive you out. You can warm yourself a bit." Yosele didn't answer.

"Why are you silent, little fool? Come more quickly," Reb Shoyel said as he tried to help him up. "Come, my child, I'm afraid you are already quite sick. Such foolishness, such foolishness! I absolutely don't understand what you were thinking when you lay down here to sleep." And Reb Shoyel tried to take his little hand to lead him away, but the desolate child was unable to stand on his feet.

"You're very sick, poor child!" the old Jew said with a heavy sigh. "What shall I do with you?"

He put his ritual slaughterer's knives in his coat and lifted Yosele into his arms. "He's as light as a three-year-old child," he said to himself.

At first Shoyel thought to take Yosele to the Tax Assessor's house, which was close by, but soon reconsidered. "No," he thought, "better to take him to someone else, although I absolutely don't have any time for this. The butchers will go crazy. So let them go crazy! What then? Leave him here in the street? What a terrible situation. I wouldn't have thought such a thing could happen."

At the first Jewish window in which he saw a light, Reb Shoyel knocked to ask that they open the door. "What a story, what a story!" Reb Shoyel groaned as he entered the house. "A child lies down to sleep under a gate on such a night, the rain pouring by bucketfuls. He has no worries and sleeps probably more deeply than a grown man. He doesn't hear at all as it rains on him, he sleeps without cares and catches a cold. And, I'm afraid, he's brought some big problems onto himself. It's a good thing I saw him! It's a long way to my house, so I considered: Jews are, after all, Jews. What Jew would not let a child who wanders the streets on such a night come into his house? So I've brought him to you."

"A Jewish child?" the man asked.

"A Jewish child, a little orphan! Last night, after Maariv, saying Kaddish for his mother. A kosher, devout soul was his mother!"

The man took a look at the child and soon recognized him. "This is that little boy that everyone calls a thief!" he said. "There's a whole story people told me about him. But that's not my problem. You see, I like the boy. Listen to my story: once, I noticed in my cheder that my boys were looking out the window for quite a while and were messing about with someone out there. I got angry with them and thought nothing of it. But what scamps boys are! One of my schoolboys deliberately poured a cup of hot tea through the window in order to burn somebody. I heard a cry and ran outside, and my heart melted! It was this very boy, burned, poor thing. I recognize him very well. I brought him into the school, took off his little pants, and, thank God, there were no blisters. The tea probably wasn't very hot. What a miracle, as I am a Jew! 'Little boy,' I asked him, 'what are you doing there under the window?'

"'I'm listening to the studying here!' he answered me.

"'What are you learning here?' I asked with curiosity. "Nu, what do you know? He reeled off a whole chapter of Isaiah by heart, exactly as I had taught it to my schoolboys. My heart ached when I was told the young boy's whole history, and you can believe me, Reb Shoyel, if I hadn't heard that on this boy's account, Reb Berl Shatz lost half his students, I would joyously have brought him into my school and taught him for free.

"I'm a newcomer here in your town, but I literally can't understand how such a child who has such a desire to learn, could find himself without a single relative to make sure he didn't fall through the cracks. Well, it was probably destined that you should find him in the street, poor thing, and bring him here to me. The Master of the Universe apparently knows that I pity him and showed you the way to my door. May this be accorded to you as a mitzvah, 'it is given to a good person to act justly.'"

"In truth, I had no other intention than to bring my little treasure to Reb Shloyme, our Tax Assessor," Reb Shoyel admitted. "But on the way I recalled the whole history of what happened to this same boy thanks to Reb Shloyme's wife, and I had this thought as I went along: perhaps this would be a test from Above falling on our Tax Assessor, and he would surely pass by doing the right thing. But then I figured it was inadvisable to take such a chance with the boy's life.

"And so I brought him here to you. Let him warm his little bones! Ask your wife to dress him warmly, perhaps he'll be able to sweat it out and become healthy. When it's time for prayers, I'll make an announcement in the *besmedresh*. You'll see, Jews won't let such a thing happen to him again! If one can just rouse a Jew's conscience, then everything will be all right! 'The people of *Yisroel* are required to give.' A collection must be taken up; a Jew shouldn't be a shirker!"

"But a good payer, Reb Shoyel, shouldn't wait until he's asked for money," said the Vilna Rebbe. "He himself remembers his own debt, and even before anyone comes to collect, he brings his payment right to the collector's house. And that's been our defect forever! We Jews don't have within ourselves the inspiration; there has to be a debt collector to awaken the attention every time there is a need. Wouldn't it be better to forestall evils so they don't come at all?"

"You are too young, Reb Betsalel," Reb Shoyel said. "'One may not add debts to Jews.' Times are hard these days. We must thank the Master of the Universe that Jews are still able to pay up when payment is demanded; these are also great miracles."

Meanwhile, the teacher's wife had removed Yosele's wet garments, had laid him in the bed, and dressed him warmly. But he was so fevered and delirious, she had been unable to understand one word out of him.

"A dead child," she told the men with terror in her eyes. "God knows if he will live through the day. Someone should run for a doctor. Perhaps the boy can still be saved!"

"Please run to the slaughterhouse, Reb Betsalel, and ask the butchers to send for my son-in-law to do the killing today. I'll run and bring Nakhmen the Assistant Surgeon."

In a few minutes, Reb Shoyel returned with Reb Nakhmen, who soon determined that Yosele had contracted a severe lung inflammation and was in grave danger. His advice was to take the boy as quickly as possible to the poorhouse where there is always a doctor and an apothecary on hand. "This is no place for him," said the Assistant Surgeon. "Unless one gets him a doctor and medicine, he could be in even greater danger."

Not waiting a minute, old Reb Shoyel picked up the sick child and held him in his arms the way you carry a baby to a bris. The Vilna teacher's wife had already wrapped Yosele in a warm blanket and, with tears in her eyes, said, "Go, Reb Shoyel, every minute counts, save the poor child! Thanks to his mother's merits, God will send true relief to him through you! Here, I'll just dress my children, wash them, and say the blessings with them. Then I'll come immediately to the poorhouse to be near him. My heart is overflowing with compassion."

"I am a day laborer," said the teacher. "I must pray and then run to the school, but I don't want to let you, Reb Shoyel, take him in your own arms. I'm younger and it will certainly be easier for me than for you."

"He is no heavy burden, Reb Betsalel," insisted Reb Shoyel. "What a scarred, tortured little body, poor thing. He weighs as much as a three-year-old child. May it be as easy to save him as it will be for me to carry him to the poorhouse."

# Thirteen

Yosele lay three days in the poorhouse. Besides old Reb Shoyel the Butcher, who used to come a few times a day to visit, the Vilna teacher's wife often came to sit for hours, adjusting the little pillow under his head, giving him his medicine, and showing him the same devotion a mother gives her own child. Nobody else came to see him; nobody else was interested in him.

His own father, who was in the same poorhouse under the same roof, didn't know his own miserable child was lying near him in such danger. Borekh the Sexton was at that time dangerously ill himself, and who would think of laying such upsetting news on him in his condition?

It was on the third day that Yoyne the Water Carrier first found out, in Sheyndele's kitchen, what had happened to Yosele. The cook told him she'd heard in the butcher's shop that Khyene's boy had been found frozen in the street and that he lies now, dangerously ill, in the poorhouse.

Yoyne didn't wait. With his empty buckets in both hands he ran straight to the poorhouse. Running past the home of Getsl the Women's Tailor, he went in to see if Sorele knew anything. But Sorele knew nothing. On Shabbes she'd searched for her little brother the whole day, but couldn't find him. The old sexton at the Chassidic prayer house had said that Yosele hadn't slept there for several nights.

"Come, Sorele, quickly, to the poorhouse," Yoyne said breathlessly, seeing that she knew nothing. "Come."

"Is it father, perhaps?" Sorele asked in terror, fearing the awful words "sick" or "dead."

"It's not your father; it's Yosele. He's sick, poor thing. They say he's very sick and has been lying in the poorhouse for three days."

"A bullet has fallen on me," the twelve-year-old girl cried. "Thunder has struck me! Oy, I'm guilty myself. He got sick through hunger and cold before I could give him his portion of my food! Oy, my poor little brother, my poor Yosele, my heart, the apple of my eye."

Breathlessly they both entered the poorhouse, both falling onto Yosele's little cot. The Vilna teacher's wife was sitting nearby, sadly watching the miserable child's suffering.

"Yosele, my little brother, my heart!" cried Sorele, and an ocean of tears fell over the sick child. But Yosele didn't hear, or already didn't have the strength to respond.

"Yosele, answer me, please! Sorele, your grieving, bitter sister, stands here beside you. Answer, Yosele, do you recognize me?" She sobbed and with a heartrending cry woke her little brother. The boy opened his eyes, gave a blind and empty look, and soon closed them again.

"If we could only speak one word to each other, Yosele, my crown, just one word for your wretched sister. Yosele, open your eyes. My little brother, see how I stand here beside you! My heart, my little brother, please look at me!"

Once again, Yosele opened his eyes. Sorele fell on him and kissed him with such devotion, as if her kisses could cure his illness or take it from him into herself.

"My little brother, my little orphan, just survive, my dear Yosele! Be healthy, my miserable little soul. I've bought you a *Svarbe!* You've wanted to study and you can! Just live, Yosele. I won't leave you. I won't be parted from you! I'll care for you like my eye, my heart, my life! You'll be with me, Yosele, or I'll be with you in the street. We'll wander together under the empty sky until God sees our suffering!

"Have pity, God in Heaven! Give my little brother health, send him a cure, or take me instead of him, our mother's only consolation, her pride and joy to her very last minute. Oy Mama, Mama, why are you silent? Why don't you pray for your dear child, for Yosele, Mama, on his sickbed!"

The Vilna teacher's wife, sitting nearby, also cried and sobbed hearing Sorele's pleas. Yosele kept his eyes open for a long while, looked at Sorele so sorrowfully, so emptily, it seemed he spoke to her. He lamented to her of his troubles, which pained him now. But soon his eyes closed and he seemed to sleep; sleeping so sweetly, he even snores.

But Reb Shoyel, approaching the bed, knew by the snoring what kind of sleep this was. He winked at Yoyne to take the women away, but Yoyne, a broken man, didn't take his eyes off the child he had really loved so much—the boy who was so dear to him that he would have given away half his life to him in an instant.

Reb Shoyel began to speak, "Women, it's time to leave him be. He's already ended his reckonings with you, paid out all his debts in his short life. Now he prepares his little soul to go back soon to where he came from. Don't hinder him. Go away now and let him die in peace. Take them out, Reb Yoyne, and bring in a light. He will soon draw his last breath."

Yoyne, who had been standing like a beaten down simpleton, woke as from a deep sleep and tore Sorele unwillingly from the little bed. He took her with his gigantic hands out of the poorhouse like a small child. The Vilna teacher's wife remained standing with Sorele in the street and helped the unlucky sister lament and cry.

Yoyne brought in a couple of small candles, lit them, gave one to Reb Shoyel, and holding one himself with tears in his eyes, they awaited the boy's last breath.

Yosele didn't suffer much. His whole life had been a kind of waning before death, and he died more easily than he had lived.

"'Blessed is the True Judge,'" Reb Shoyel pronounced and pressed shut the half-opened eyes.

In an hour's time, Yosele was already removed from the poorhouse. The funeral procession was only a few men: Reb Shoyel, Reb Yoyne, Getsl the Women's Tailor, and a couple of sextons, in addition to the one who carried Yosele in a child's coffin across his shoulder with a leather strap.

None of the town's women but the Vilna teacher's wife and Sorele followed Yosele. Sorele tried with all her strength to free herself from the woman's hand. She wanted to tear her little brother from the sexton who was carrying away her heart, her crown, to the place from which no one returns.

"Let me go to my brother," she shrieked. "He's still alive! He's not dead. He can't be dead. People always told lies about him, and this is a lie, too! He's not dead. Oy, let me go. No, I won't let him lie, so young, in the earth."

The sexton had to hold her back from the coffin because the Vilna teacher's wife had no strength left to restrain her.

When Yosele was laid in the ground, Sorele, wailing, tore away wildly and fell to the open grave. "My little brother, my Yosele! Oy, people, see how beautiful he is! He still lives! Have pity, give him to me. I don't have anything left in my life, nothing!"

"Enough crying, enough lamenting, my child!" Reb Shoyel said, taking her by the hand. "Your little brother is dead. He died as a pure, clean soul. Let his rites be performed, and be consoled: it's not some thief that's being buried here, but a holy little soul, who, from the day of his birth to his dying day, suffered for the sins of others, for the evils of others! A better one shall he be for you and for the people Yisroel!"

Two big tears, which had this whole time shone as if frozen in the eyes of the pious old Jew, fell at last, rolling down Reb Shoyel's sunken cheeks, over his snow white beard, straight into the open grave.

Yoyne the Water Carrier, looking at Reb Shoyel, also cried, and it was hard for Reb Shoyel to silence him.

"Perhaps I am guilty for his young death!" Yoyne sobbed. "Such a child, such a kosher, pious child! He shines from the grave like a little angel! Forgive me, Yosele. I didn't mean, God forbid, to do wrong by you!"

That evening in the *besmedresh*, Reb Yoyne said Kaddish at Maariv.

"A yortzeit, Yoyne?" members of the congregation asked him.

"No, not a yortzeit, I'm saying Kaddish for Khyene the Preacher's daughter."

"Who is supposed to be saying Kaddish for her? Who is her Kaddish?"

"Her Kaddish is already with her in Paradise!"

"Khyene's little boy? That little thief, you mean, Reb Yoyne?"

Yoyne didn't answer and left the besmedresh.

The men there did not understand Yoyne. They shrugged their shoulders and answered, "He's probably drunk!"

The next day, when the cook told Sheyndele that Khyene's little boy, the thief, died the previous day in the poorhouse, Sheyndele answered: "It's absolutely better to be laid young in the grave than to sit later in prison. May he suffer, Master of the Universe, instead of my dear child, my only son Leybele, may he live to be a hundred and twenty years!"

# ACKNOWLEDGEMENTS

My sincerest thanks to Jane Peppler for her marvelous work in translating Jacob Dinezon's *Yosele* into English. Thanks also to Sheva Zucker and Curt Leviant for their suggestions on the translation, and to Arthur Clark, Lisa Waldo, and Cathy Levinson for their proofreading assistance.

I also wish to express my deep appreciation to Robin and Jim Evans and Carolyn Toben for their ongoing love and support.

Scott Hilton Davis
February 2015

# GLOSSARY

*Ayzenharts.* Iron heart.

*besmedresh.* A house of prayer and study.

*bimah.* The raised platform or pulpit in the synagogue on which the Torah scroll is placed for public reading and where the service leader often stands.

*bris.* The ceremony of circumcision performed on a Jewish boy when he is eight days old.

*challah.* A braided bread eaten on the Sabbath and holidays.

*Chassid.* A follower of the Chassidic movement.

*Chassidim.* The followers of Chassidism, a mystical Jewish religious movement founded in the eighteenth century in Eastern Europe.

*cheder.* Traditional religious elementary school.

*chuppah.* The canopy under which the bride and groom stand during the wedding ceremony.

*Esau.* The oldest son of Isaac and brother of Jacob in the Bible; a man of the field, unsophisticated, and rough.

*Gehennah.* Hell.

*Gemara.* The portion of the Talmud that provides rabbinical commentary on the Mishnah.

*gevalt.* An expression of alarm, anxiety, or shock.

*groschen.* An Austrian coin; one-hundredth part of a shilling.

*goy.* A Gentile; a non-Jew.

*Kaddish.* The mourner's prayer for the dead.

*Khumesh with Rashi.* The five books of the Torah with commentary by "Rashi," the acronym for Rabbi Shlomo Yitskhaki (1040-1105 CE).

*kopeck.* A Russian coin; one-hundredth part of a ruble.

*kosher.* Foods or other products that conform to Jewish dietary law.

*lulav.* A palm branch used during the Sukkot service.

*Maariv.* The evening prayer service.

*mazl tov.* Congratulations.

*melamed.* A teacher of children.

*mezuzah.* A small parchment scroll inscribed with religious texts and attached in a case to the doorpost of a Jewish home.

*minyan.* Ten men needed to hold a public Jewish prayer service.

*Mincha.* The afternoon prayer service.

*Mishnah.* The first compilation of the Jewish oral law or "Oral Torah."

*mitzvah.* A commandment or good deed.

*Moydeh Ani.* A prayer of thanksgiving recited immediately upon waking.

*rebbe.* Teacher. "Rebbe" may also be the title of a Chassidic rabbi. By contrast, the term "Reb" is simply "Mister," and a term of respect for any adult male.

*rebbetzin.* The rebbe's wife.

*ruble.* A Russian coin.

*Rosh Hashanah.* The Jewish New Year.

*sexton.* The *"shammes"* or caretaker of the study house or synagogue.

*Shabbes.* The Sabbath.

*Shacharit.* The morning prayer service.

*Shema Yisroel.* Words taken from the Torah that form a central prayer in the morning and evening prayer services.

*shivah.* The formal mourning period of seven days during which friends visit the home of the deceased to comfort the bereaved.

*shlepper.* A foolish or stupid person.

*shtetl.* A small Jewish town or village in Eastern Europe.

*shul.* A synagogue or house of prayer.

*Shulkhan Arukh.* A compilation of Jewish legal codes by the Sephardic Rabbi Joseph Caro in the mid-1500s.

*Svarbe.* A volume containing the twenty-four books of the Hebrew Bible. In Yiddish, Svarbe is the contraction of the Hebrew words esrim-ve-arbe or twenty-four.

*Talmud.* The collection of Jewish law and tradition consisting of the Mishnah and the Gemara.

*Talmudist.* Someone who studies the Talmud.

*Talmud-Torah.* The traditional, tuition-free elementary school maintained by the community for the poorest students.

*Torah.* The first five books of the Hebrew Bible.

*treyf.* Not kosher.

*tzaddik.* A saint or righteous person.

*yeshiva.* Jewish institute of higher Talmudic learning.

*Yiddishkayt.* Jewishness; Jewish culture.

*Yisroel.* Israel.

*Yom Kippur.* The Day of Atonement.

*yortzeit.* The anniversary of a death.

*zogerin.* A women prayer leader in the women's section of the synagogue.

# About the Translator

Jane Peppler graduated from Yale University with a degree in Russian language and literature. She began singing Yiddish songs in 1983 and directed the Triangle Jewish Chorale in North Carolina for fourteen years. Peppler studies with Yiddish professor and textbook author, Sheva Zucker, and has attended two intensive summer Yiddish courses at the Medem Bibliotheque in Paris.

In addition to translating Yiddish stories by Sholem Aleichem, Ayzik Meyer Dik, and Mendele Moykher Sforim, Peppler has completed English translations of Jacob Dinezon's *Yosele, Alter,* and *Hershele.*

In 2014, Peppler published *Yiddish Songs from Warsaw 1929-1934: The Itsik Zhelonek Collection.* She has also produced and performed on several albums of Yiddish music, including "I Can't Complain (But Sometimes I Still Do)," "Cabaret Warsaw: Yiddish and Polish Hits of the 1920s-1930s," and the three volume set, "Yiddish Songs from Warsaw."

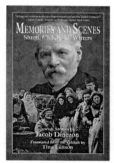